A Cowboy's Big Dream

SWEET VIEW RANCH

BOOK TEN

JESSIE GUSSMAN

Contents

Acknowledgments

Cover art by Julia Gussman
Editing by Heather Hayden
Narration by Jay Dyess
Author Services by CE Author Assistant

~

Listen to the unabridged audio for FREE performed by Jay Dyess on the Say with Jay channel on YouTube. Get early access to all of Jay's recordings and listen to Jessie's books before they're available to the general public, plus get daily Bible readings by Jay and bonus scenes by becoming a Say with Jay channel member.

Chapter One

ooper Cordray looked around the small cabin. It wasn't much, but he didn't need much. Not anymore. Although, this wasn't anything like what he'd grown used to. Still, it was bigger than what he'd grown up in.

He set his bag and suitcase down and walked back out to his truck to grab his guitar.

Of the three things, his guitar was the thing he couldn't live without. Even before he became a superstar country singer, his guitar had gotten him through a lot of hard things that might have made someone else, someone who didn't have music, give up.

As he had done over the course of his life, he pondered the idea of music and how odd it was that human beings were the only creatures on earth who enjoyed something so arbitrary and abstract. It brought out strong emotions and swept people away. And people didn't just love to listen to it, but to see it performed in real time held a fascination that could not be explained. Plus, there was something even more stirring about actually creating the music to begin with.

Nothing else in the world compared.

Lord, why did You give me that gift only to snatch it away?

He didn't really mean that though. God hadn't snatched his gift away. God had just snatched his music and the career that had taken him a decade of dedication and commitment and hard work and daily grind to build.

And it had taken the Lord to build that, too, because there were tons of people who had worked just as hard as he had and hadn't seen the success that he did. He knew, beyond a shadow of a doubt, that without God, his career wouldn't have been possible.

Still, he had been at the pinnacle, was just finding out the height that he could actually reach, when everything came crashing down.

Lord, why?

As usual, there was no answer, and he grabbed the guitar out of the back of the truck, slamming the door shut, walking back to the cabin.

It might be small, but it was the cabin his agent had booked for the next six months, and this was the cabin that he would use.

He had heard that North Dakota winters were brutal, but he had been assured that he would stay nice and snug in this cabin. He had also been assured that someone would take care of his laundry, get groceries for him, and he would be welcome to eat meals at the big farmhouse if he so chose.

He didn't want to see anyone, so he wasn't going to the farmhouse for anything, not even food. Although...he didn't cook, so it could get interesting. He had been warned that North Dakota winters could make a person feel isolated, and he might want the company, but right now, all he wanted was to hole up and be left alone.

The cabin was divided into two areas. The kitchen/dining room/living room area on one side, and the bedroom/master bath on the other side.

It was new and smelled like fresh wood and cleaning products, and he took a deep breath.

Yeah, this would be just perfect for him. There was a fireplace in the living room, gas, and one in the bedroom as well. The bed had way more pillows than he would ever use, and he decided that when the housekeeper showed up, he would ask her to remove all but two. He would only use one to sleep with, but if he ever sat on his bed, he might need a second one for his back. Beyond that, the other pillows were a nuisance.

He set his guitar at the foot of the bed, along with his suitcase and traveling bag, and walked back out to the living room.

A comfortable-looking loveseat and a recliner both faced the fireplace. A small table sat in front of the window with the view of green grass blowing in the wind. Being that it was early September, the temperature outside was warm, if not hot, the way it would be in Tennessee, or rural Virginia where he had been raised, this time of year. In the mountains, it got cold at night, but the temperature climbed to quite warm during the day, with no humidity.

It was his mother's favorite time of year. She always said the sky was bluest in September, and the air was pure, with the scent of winter on the wind.

He didn't know about that, but the air in the mountains generally smelled different than the air in Nashville.

Neither one of them smelled anything like the air in North Dakota. It had a wildness all its own.

He liked the little front porch of the cabin as well, although he didn't go back out but walked slowly to the kitchen, his fingers trailing over the small table which had four chairs but barely enough room for two people.

Anything bigger would have taken up too much space, since the kitchen was a nice size for such a tiny cabin. It had nice countertops. They looked like granite and expensive. There was a full oven, a large refrigerator, and a good-sized microwave over the stove.

The housekeeper was supposed to do his laundry, so he didn't bother looking for a washer and dryer, since he knew there weren't any.

This was going to be his home for the next six months. This was where he was going to...heal? He didn't know if he was going to heal so much as he wanted to write revenge songs. Pour out his heart on the page, and in the next six months, he wanted to create music that would crush the music that had been stolen from him.

His hands folded into fists, and he lifted his head, looking out at the peaceful scenery once more. He was not going to think about it. He'd spent enough time in the last three weeks ruminating over what Regina Blue had done to him.

Regina, whom he had thought was his friend. Who perhaps might have become more. Who he had shared secrets with. Collaborated with, first in the duets that he had written, then sharing snippets of songs he was writing, getting her opinion on them, asking if she thought anything could be made into a duet that they could tour with again next year, since their duet tour had been so successful this year. It was the highest-grossing tour of all time.

Except, Regina Blue had been working behind his back the entire time to rip him off.

His jaw clenched. He wasn't going to think about it anymore, but all roads seemed to lead to that end. She had betrayed him, she had stolen from him, she had taken what he had given her and trashed it completely. He had trusted her, and she had betrayed that trust.

He would never trust anyone again. Ever.

His phone buzzed, startling him out of his thoughts. There he was again, sinking down into the negative. That's not what he wanted for this time. He was done with that. He grabbed his phone and noted that the text was from his publicist.

> Hope you're settled in. The housekeeper will
> be contacting you shortly to set things up to
> your satisfaction.

> Okay, thanks.

He looked around the tiny cabin again. He really didn't have too much to say to the housekeeper. He wanted her to bother him as little as possible. Of course, by the time he'd been here by himself for three or four months, maybe he would be ready for some company. The thought of spending the holidays by himself didn't sit well, but the thought of spending them with the public, or even with his own family, didn't sit well either. All anyone wanted to talk about was what had happened with Regina Blue, and that's the one thing he didn't want to talk about. Ever.

He hadn't taken a day off in months, and so he found himself drawn to the rocking chairs on the front porch, sitting down and facing the southern sky as the sun sank on the western horizon. It was a beautiful view, calm and peaceful, and the cabin was situated in such a way that while there were other cabins nearby—he'd seen them as he pulled in—they weren't in sight. It was clever the way it was laid out, and he appreciated the foresight of the people who designed it. Perhaps they too sometimes needed privacy. A place where they could heal.

He was thinking about getting his guitar out and strumming a few chords, maybe singing a song that he had written a while ago or an old hymn, or perhaps working on a new song, when his phone buzzed again.

> Welcome to Sweet View Ranch. I'm Priscilla Clybourn, and I'll be your housekeeper while you're here. I'd like to come chat with you whenever it's convenient so we can set up some boundaries and you can let me know the schedule you'd like me to keep. Just reply when you have time, no rush. I can meet pretty much any time.

Priscilla. What a name. Wasn't that something people named their kids in the 1800s?

He didn't think he knew another Priscilla in his entire friend set, which was quite extensive. Far more extensive than it had been growing up in the backwoods of Virginia.

He tried to stop thinking about her name and focus on her message. What would be the best thing to set up? When would he be least likely to be bothered by her?

He did some of his best writing in the morning as the sun was coming up, and he also enjoyed watching the sunset. For now, he'd be sitting outside on the porch in the evening, so it would not be a good time for her to come, but come winter, he would be inside, almost certainly.

He didn't know what to tell her. But maybe he could think about it until she arrived.

> I'll be here. Come whenever you want.

There. He really didn't care. And that was part of his problem. He'd stopped caring about anything. Except getting revenge and the pain and suffering that Regina Blue had put him through. The pain from the way she'd treated him and what she'd stolen from him. He couldn't get it back. He'd tried, and he lost. Which was frustrating, because it had been his, but it was his word against hers, and she had won.

He wasn't sure what he was expecting, but less than five minutes later, a four-wheeler rumbled over the hill, and a woman, her long hair blowing out behind her, drove up at a reasonable speed and parked behind his pickup.

She sat on the four-wheeler for a moment after she shut it off, looking at the sunset and then looking back at him.

"You must be Cooper?" she asked, like she didn't recognize him. Maybe she was the one person in the world who had been living under a rock for the last three years, and maybe she truly didn't know who he was.

"Yes, ma'am," he said, his upbringing coming out in his words and his voice. His grandma would have had him cut a switch from the willow tree out back if he hadn't added the "ma'am" onto the "yes."

"I'm Priscilla." She dismounted from the ATV and walked over to the front porch, stepping up and holding out her hand. "Welcome to Sweet View Ranch."

He looked at her hand for a moment, long fingers, much longer than he would expect on a woman who was on the shorter side of average. Piano-playing fingers is what his grandma would have said.

He stood slowly, adjusting his hat, before grasping her fingers and giving her hand a perfunctory pump.

"Nice to meet you. Have a seat," he said, nodding at the other rocking chair.

"Thank you," Priscilla said, sounding slightly surprised.

"My pleasure, ma'am," he said. Although, it really wasn't his pleasure. He wanted to get rid of her. He wanted to be alone.

"All right," she said as soon as her butt touched the seat, like she didn't want to stay any longer than she had to. "I don't want to keep you, but when your agent booked this, it was with the understanding that someone would be doing your laundry and grocery shopping and possibly cooking your meals as well. I just wanted to make sure that the schedule as we set it up suits you."

"I appreciate your consideration, ma'am."

"Of course. And don't think that this is set in stone. If what we decide this evening doesn't work in the future at any time, you can change it. My job is to make sure you're satisfied and happy here."

The lady had a classy way of moving that drew Cooper's eye, despite himself. She sat with her hands folded in her lap, those long fingers tapered and still. Her ankles crossed and her feet tucked under the chair, she sat with her back straight, not touching the back of the chair.

She didn't look uncomfortable, just...classy and almost queenly.

"I guess I don't really care. Right now, it's nice out and I can come outside while you're working inside, but at some point, we're going to be bumping into each other, because it will be cold and I'm not leaving the cabin for you to clean it."

"I totally understand. I want to stay out of your way as much as possible. But if you don't care, I can adjust my cleaning schedule to whatever works."

"We could try afternoons."

"That would be fine. It usually takes me about two hours to clean. I have a second set of sheets, so I'll be able to change your bed while I'm doing it and we won't have to wait for the laundry."

"All right." He hadn't even considered that. "I assume you bring your towels then too?"

"I will. Typically, I leave four towels here for the week and bring four clean ones when I clean. If that isn't sufficient, you can just let me know."

"That sounds fine." He wasn't even sure he was going to shower. Didn't feel like it. If he wasn't going out, it wouldn't matter if he didn't shower, didn't shave, didn't do anything that normal people thought was essential for living.

"I can shop whenever you want to. I'd like to have a set day if possible, but I certainly am not going to be legalistic about it, if we need to change it."

"It shouldn't matter. I don't have any groceries right now. So whatever day today is, I guess tomorrow would be a good day for groceries." He ran a hand over his face, thinking this was too much stuff for him to consider.

"All right then. Just send me a list of what you want me to get. Every once in a while if I'm running into town in the middle of the week, I can pick you up anything you'd like. I'll just shoot you a text and ask. I suppose the main thing is, it's a bit of a drive, and I don't want to be going every day."

"I understand."

He wanted this meeting to be over. It had already lasted longer than his tolerance for people. Except, the woman was sweet and nice. And she smelled good too.

"And I believe that you've already been told, but the invitation is always available for you to eat at the farmhouse. When we have people at the dude ranch, there is a bonfire every evening, and there's a meal at the bunkhouse at noon. When the season's over, and we don't have any guests on the ranch, we still have meals at the bunkhouse with the Clybourn family, and you're welcome. Sometime when you want, I can show you where the bunkhouse is, or you can just wander around and ask whoever you run into, and they'll be happy to point you to it."

That seemed kind of casual, but he nodded. "I appreciate it."

"All right. I'll set cleaning for Monday afternoons, and groceries will be Friday afternoons. If you need anything, you have my number, just text me."

"I'll do that, ma'am. Thanks."

"All right. Enjoy your stay." She pushed off from the rocking chair, gave him a last smile, and if he had been listening to his gram's voice in his head, he would have stood up out of respect for her. But he did not. He just wanted her to go. So he could be alone.

She made him think about things and feel things that he didn't want to. He thought it was probably anyone, anyone who would be nice and kind and sweet.

The idea made a melody trickle through his brain. He watched as she walked with confidence and casual class back to the four-wheeler. Somehow it seemed like she should be getting in a golden carriage.

Four-wheeler or carriage, she conducted herself with class. She was the kind of girl who wanted marriage. Phrases started swirling in his head, and his fingers itched for his guitar and a pen.

He barely waited until the four-wheeler was out of sight before he hurried into the cabin and got both, coming back out to the porch to the blaze of the sunset.

That was the first that he had even considered writing since the blowup with Regina Blue. Priscilla had inspired the perfect revenge song. He'd been writing songs long enough to know that he had the start to a good one. He'd have to thank Priscilla. She helped him more than she knew.

Chapter Two

"What was he like?"

The question greeted her as soon as Priscilla set foot in the farmhouse. She had just come to collect her kids and take them to her own cabin for the evening. But she should have guessed that the family would gather around.

Mina looked especially interested. "He looks so kind and friendly when I see him on social media. And his music is just amazing. Does he match the image?" She looked expectantly at Priscilla, and Priscilla wasn't sure what to say.

"He was very polite. But it was obvious that he wanted his privacy." That was the whole reason he was there, and she felt a little bit like she was the gatekeeper. Like he wouldn't appreciate her talking about him to her family, even casual details.

She knew that there had been some kind of big thing going on with him, and she'd heard some of the details as her family talked about it, but she didn't keep up with that kind of stuff.

"I was so disappointed when he tried to steal Regina Blue's music. He acted like it was all his. I guess, I really liked his music, but I don't so much anymore." Mina lifted a shoulder and turned away.

"I didn't follow that very well. And I have no clue what's going on. Maybe that's for the best." Priscilla figured that she didn't want whatever he had done in the past to taint her opinion of him now. She was going to have to clean his house once a week, and wash his clothes, and do his grocery shopping. She didn't want to do that with some kind of chip on her shoulder because the guy didn't have any character or, maybe more accurately, made a mistake.

Lots of people made mistakes. She was the poster child for people who made mistakes. Big ones.

"I think that's probably for the best. The less you know about him, the less your opinion will be tainted, and the less you'll be tempted to talk," Alaska said, walking in with a baby on one hip and a plate of cookies in the other hand. "We made these today, and I promised your kids I would wrap some up for you guys to take home to your cabin."

She handed the plate to Priscilla.

"Just what we need, more cookies," she said, laughing and taking the plate. "Thank you. Thank you for the cookies, thank you for baking with my children. You are so sweet and a mother to everyone." Her name should have been Eve instead of Alaska.

"I have as much fun as they do, and who doesn't love cookies?"

"Right?" Priscilla said, thinking that just because she loved them didn't make them good for her. "All right, guys, put your stuff away and let's head back to the house. I can't wait to read the next chapter in *Where the Red Fern Grows*."

"Oh, yeah! Maybe we can read two tonight!" Justin said as he hurried into the room with a handful of toys he put in the toybox. The toys probably weren't his, although he might have been playing with some of the younger kids. Justin had been great with the little ones, and it made Priscilla sad to see it. She had always hoped that he would have a lot of little brothers and sisters of his own. But that wasn't the way the Lord had ordained her life, and she was grateful that he got to play with his cousins.

"Thank you for picking those things up, Justin," Alaska said, immediately noticing the boy's helpfulness.

Priscilla appreciated that. It was so easy to see the bad in someone else's kids, but Alaska seemed to look at the children and see their best qualities. It was one of the things that endeared Alaska to Priscilla. She treated her kids like they were her own.

Of course, Ezra had done the same with the children Alaska had brought to their marriage, so she did have a good example in her husband.

"Zaylee, come on." Priscilla glanced down the hall and saw Zaylee coming out with an armful of toys as well to put in the toybox.

"Thank you for helping," she said as Zaylee came over and stood beside her, a little quieter but eager to get home and back to their story as well.

Both of her kids were quite capable of reading on their own, but ever since they had moved into the cabin of their own, their special thing had been reading together each night. Sometimes she read for an hour or more, until her voice gave out.

She would be forever grateful to Ezra for his foresight in building the cabins and equipping at least one with a washer and dryer so it could be lived in full-time without the need to do a weekly laundry run. It was handy, because she could be in charge of cleaning the other six cabins, and she'd gratefully taken that on. The family had agreed that her living in the cabin would just be part of the pay that she got for working on the farm.

"How are your social media videos doing?" Alaska asked as they waited for her kids to grab their jackets and put them on. At this time of year, when the sun went down, North Dakota got chilly, and she tried to teach her children to always have a jacket. Their state was absolutely beautiful, wild and amazing, but it could also be brutal.

"They're doing pretty well. I'm getting a good many views on them, and people seem to like the laid-back, 'I'm not perfect, but I'm trying' vibe I give off."

"That's exciting," Alaska said. Priscilla knew Alaska would cheer any wins she had.

After she had gotten divorced, she had been depressed and had gained some weight. After all, she had been drowning her sorrows in food, and the idea of failing at marriage, and then the fight over the kids, and her losing that fight, had been exceptionally difficult.

When she had decided that she was going to take back control of her health and her life, she started exercising, and then based on her own inability to find exactly what she was looking for, for free, online, she decided to make her own videos.

Now that she had the cabin of her own, it was a little bit easier. Her kids cooperated since they knew she hoped to eventually make money with her videos.

She supposed if she had a big family like she had always wanted, it would have been a lot harder to have this little gig on the side. It would be harder to do anything, but that was the way it was with children. She supposed that's why so many people didn't want to have a lot, because it kept them from doing what they wanted. She looked at it slightly different, like life really wasn't supposed to be about her doing what she wanted anyway.

"Ready," her kids said, and she smiled, nodding as they opened the door and walked out into the night.

They could have ridden the four-wheeler to their house, but the walk was less than a quarter of a mile, and it was a beautiful night.

Plus, she cherished every single second she got to spend with her kids. She had been away from them enough to know that life was fragile, and unpredictable, and didn't always go the way a person thought it was going to.

"It's a pretty night," she said, with Justin on one side holding her hand and Zaylee on the other.

"You say that every night," Justin said, sounding a little bit annoyed, but she knew he agreed with her about the evening.

"I guess I've just learned that every night is a blessing. You never know if you're going to get another one. Wouldn't it be terrible if we never got to see the sky again?"

"Why wouldn't we get to see the sky again?" Zaylee asked. "It's there every night."

"And we're blessed to live in a place where we can see it well. If we lived in a city, the stars wouldn't look nearly as bright. Or you don't know what could happen tomorrow; we could have an accident where we lose our sight. And then you'd never see the stars again. And think of all the times that you would sit there and think, I used to be able to see the stars and appreciate them, but I just didn't take the time to even notice."

She didn't know if her children were old enough to understand that or not, but sometimes it didn't hurt kids to hear things that they didn't understand. Sometimes their brains would tuck ideas away until they were old enough to bring it out and examine it and put it into context.

She had certainly done that more than once with some of the things that her parents had said. Of course, losing her parents early had made their words all the more precious to her, but that was one of those unpredictable things in life. She had absolutely no intention of going anywhere, but she didn't know what God's plans were, and if tomorrow brought some tragedy that took her away from her children, she wanted them to remember this night walking home, hand in hand with their mom, appreciating the wonder of the universe and the loving God who made it.

"There's the Big Dipper," Justin said, pointing to the Big Dipper which was in the same position it had been each night they had walked home. She smiled, happy he pointed it out on his own.

"Mom?" Zaylee said, after they had taken another step or two.

"Yes?"

"Is it always going to be like this?"

She wasn't sure exactly what her daughter was saying. She figured the best thing to do was just ask. "Like what?"

"Us. Here. I mean, we were in Wyoming with Dad, and we didn't get to see you much, and now we're here, and…is it going to end?"

Priscilla took a deep breath. This was what happened to her daughter because her parents' marriage had ended, and then her dad's marriage to the next woman had ended, and the visits to North Dakota had ended, and then living in Wyoming had ended, so in general her young life had not been steady or consistent.

Priscilla wished she could give a reassurance that it would never end, but unfortunately, life was like that at times.

"I guess that's what we were just saying, wasn't it? That sometimes we don't expect things to happen. Sometimes there are good things, like moving here to North Dakota and getting to be with me and all of your cousins was a really good thing, wasn't it?"

"Yes. It was the best thing that happened in a really long time," Zaylee said, and Priscilla sighed, although she didn't say anything. She didn't want to talk badly about her ex-husband or her children's father, but both of her kids had said that they had asked their dad if they could live with their mom, and he had told them no multiple times. They had both been relieved when they had finally been able to do it.

"And I suppose that's the way life is. Good things happen, bad things happen, and things change. We don't want them to, we want them to stay the same, but if everything just stayed like this, we would never have winter, we'd never have the new growth in spring. We would get tired of living in fall all the time. Wouldn't we?" she asked her kids.

"I wish it were summertime, because then we wouldn't have school. Although, homeschooling is better than going to school."

Priscilla laughed. "We've only been homeschooling for a week. It's probably going to get just as old as going to school, but...maybe not."

"I don't mind it. I miss my friends at school, but now I have cousins to play with. That, and I have a whole pile of things I want to do on the ranch. I can't do any of that stuff if I'm in school."

"No. But we have to balance doing fun things with doing hard things. I guess that's kind of the way life is. Balance. We always have changes, sometimes the changes are good, sometimes the changes are bad, but we have to deal with what we get. And God always knows what He's doing. Even when things seem bad, they work out for good."

Her kids didn't say anything to that, and she figured they were probably too little to understand. She hadn't really understood until something really terrible had happened to her. Her divorce.

She had never thought that she would be divorced. She thought she would be married forever, the way her parents had been until they passed away. She expected to have a big family. She expected to live near her folks, and have lots of kids, and lots of laughter, and understand that life wasn't going to be all peaches and cream, but she thought she was ready for whatever came. She just hadn't expected one of those non-peaches and cream things to be her husband cheating and her getting a divorce and losing her kids and...so many bad things.

But now, now that she was on the other side of it, she could see how God had changed her and grown her and worked things out for her good and His glory. Even though there were scars on her children, because sin always leaves scars. There were scars on her too, which didn't bother her quite as much. It was the pain her children had suffered. But it would make them stronger, better people. She was sure of it.

"We don't have to get baths tonight, do we?" Justin asked as they stepped up on the porch.

Ezra and Tobias had planned the cabins in such a way that she couldn't see the cabin where Cooper Cordray was staying, but she glanced in that direction anyway as she stepped up.

"I think you probably should. Anytime you are outside playing and getting all scruffy, it's good to get the dirt washed off of you."

He had been through a lot of hurt and pain too. She wasn't even sure he was a Christian, whether he would see pain as God using it, working it for his good, or not. But maybe that was part of the reason why she had gone through what she had. So she could help others.

"You need to hurry," Justin said to Zaylee as he opened the door. "The longer we take to get baths, the shorter time Mom has to read."

"I don't want you to hurry so much that you don't get clean," she said, walking in and smiling as she saw the schoolbooks neatly stacked in the corner. She didn't think she was ever going to get to homeschool her children. She had thought that was a dream that had evaporated along with her marriage. And yet, God had worked everything out in such a way that she couldn't be happier. The cabin, the ranch having the money to build the cabin, and Ezra planning to build one of the six cabins with two bedrooms, two baths, and a washer and dryer.

Whether it was her brother's foresight, or whether it was just God orchestrating things, she wasn't sure, but she supposed most of the credit belonged to the Lord. After all, he'd given her the brothers.

"All right. Justin, you go first, and, Zaylee, you take these cookies and put them on the counter and we'll have them tomorrow when we take a break from school in the morning."

Zaylee nodded and took the cookies, walking them to the counter as Priscilla had asked, while Priscilla grabbed her phone and looked at the text that had come in while they were walking.

Cooper had sent his list of groceries, and she needed to remember:

this was one of her new weekly responsibilities. Maybe they would need to adjust things in the winter depending on how the snowstorms came in, but she figured they would have enough time for that. Cooper didn't seem like he was a terribly unreasonable person, although she had figured that being that he was a superstar, he was used to people doing whatever he wanted. And making impossible things happen.

He was just going to have to understand that now he was dealing with a divorced mom of two children, and she didn't have miracles at her fingertips.

She almost laughed at that. If she had miracles at her fingertips, she would probably have done a lot of things that would have messed everything up. Because in hindsight, everything that God had ordained had been absolutely perfect.

Except for the divorce. She hated that stigma next to her name. But it was done and over with, and there was nothing she could do to erase it now. God didn't see her mistakes, why should she hold it against herself?

And it wasn't like she asked her husband to cheat on her or anything. He had done that himself.

The idea of reconciliation wasn't something that he had proposed or accepted when she had. He wasn't interested in getting back together. He was interested in moving on.

In her defense, no one had told her or warned her about him when they got married. She had done everything right, asked her parents' permission, asked them what they thought of him, and tried to make sure that she was doing the Lord's will. Had she misunderstood God's leading?

All those questions were pointless at this point. Except, if she had misunderstood, she didn't want to make the same mistake again.

Not that she had any intentions of getting married again. She wasn't looking, wasn't interested, and if God wanted her to get married again, he was going to have to be very, very clear about it. She was content with her cabin and her kids and her extended family on the ranch and doing whatever she could to support them and make a little extra money for herself. In her opinion, life was very, very good. And she had no desire to upset the apple cart.

Even as she thought that, she considered the conversation she just had with her children on the way home that evening. Changes happened, good and bad, and all a person could do was know that they were going to happen and do their best, looking to the Lord for guidance.

Chapter Three

A knock at the door caused Cooper to raise his head from where he sat at the kitchen table, his guitar in his lap and notebook in front of him.

Since he'd had those bits of a song the night before after seeing the housekeeper, Priscilla, he hadn't had anything else pop into his head. No matter how hard he worked on it.

Seeing that it was already afternoon, he leaned the guitar against the wall and walked over to answer the door. It was probably the woman with his groceries.

He tried not to be frustrated as he opened the door, wanting her gone as soon as possible so he could get back to work. Part of what he intended to accomplish in the six months that he was out was to write the ten best songs of his life, and if he happened to write more, he would either record them himself or sell the rights to them. But he intended to show the world that what Regina Blue took from him wasn't anything compared to what he could actually do.

"Good afternoon. I hope I'm not bothering you, but I have your groceries. I texted?"

He hadn't even noticed.

"I'm sorry. When I work, I sometimes get a one-track mind. Come on in." He stepped back as she walked in, carrying a handful of bags in each hand. "Are there more?"

"There is a little bit more, but I can do it. You go do whatever you were doing. I don't want to interrupt you."

"No. It's fine. I'll go out and grab the rest of them."

He walked out to her car, a small SUV. He assumed that an SUV was necessary in the North Dakota winter, if one planned to get around at all. Which he did not. As long as Priscilla was bringing his groceries and as long as he could work on writing his songs, he had no need to do anything else.

Of course, he wasn't big on cooking, so he ordered mostly stuff that he could make without too much problem. He'd already looked into meal services, and nothing delivered out this far, which shot the one idea that he had completely out.

By the time he came back in, she had the groceries arranged on the counter and was taking the refrigerated items out and setting them beside the refrigerator.

"I wasn't sure whether you wanted me to put them away or not, but these things need to be refrigerated ASAP."

"Thanks. If you want to put the refrigerated stuff away and anything that needs to be frozen, you can. Let the rest of it sit. I'm good with that."

"Sure," she said, taking the butter and milk out of the bags and opening the refrigerator door.

She wore a pair of yoga pants and a T-shirt that wasn't bulky but didn't hug her form, but there was something graceful in the way that she moved, like the way a ballerina moved sometimes, and his eyes followed her form.

You bring beauty and grace into my life.

The line slipped into his head.

Strong strength that bends. Not breaks.

He hummed a bit under his breath, fitting that line in with the first.

Sweetness wrapped in everyday work.

Where up until that point in the day he had had nothing at all in his mind, melodies started rapping around along with words.

It was like when she was there, his brain just opened up the floodgates and everything fell through.

"Is there anything else you need?" she asked as she brushed her hands down her pants.

He shook his head, distracted, and then said, "No, ma'am. Thank you."

"Sure. If you need anything before Monday, let me know. Otherwise, I'll be in to clean and do your laundry." She paused for just a moment. "If you want to leave your laundry out in a basket on the porch, I can pick it up Monday morning and have it washed and dried and folded and ready for you Monday afternoon. Otherwise, I have to make an additional visit to bring your clean laundry back."

"Yeah. Text me, and I'll have it out."

He wanted to get the lyrics in his head down before they left him. After the morning of absolute nothing, everything that he was getting now felt like a gift, and he wanted to write down as much as possible as soon as he could.

She walked out, and he didn't even hear her drive away, he was so busy scribbling down everything that had come into his mind while she was there.

Then, there was nothing. And he was left with a third of a song, a string of melody, and no ideas forthcoming.

Chapter Four

By Monday, Cooper was sure of two things. He was sick of eating his own cooking, and he was definitely looking forward to Priscilla coming again. He hadn't had a single thought worth writing down since the housekeeper had walked out on Friday, and he was curious to see if the wealth of ideas would come flowing when she was there again.

Not to mention, he was hungry. The groceries he had gotten were good for a week or so, but if he was going to make his own meals, he was going to need some help. He'd looked online at different videos, but they were going to take ingredients he didn't have or pots and pans he wasn't sure how to use. He just...needed some guidance.

He wondered if he would be able to hire Priscilla to give him a hand.

Part of him didn't want to ask, because she was more than likely going to suggest that he go eat supper with her family as she had invited him to do the first day he was there.

It wasn't something he was eager to do. In fact, he definitely did not want to do that. Too many people and he wasn't ready to face the many questions that were sure to be hurled at him.

He found himself pacing and checking his emails.

He hadn't checked them since he had gotten there, had silenced all the notifications on the phone, and after glancing through and seeing that he had emails from his publicist and emails from different organizations and venues, all wanting something from him, he shut his phone without opening any of them.

It seemed like every time he met someone, all they wanted was to get what they could from him. Regina Blue came to mind, but she was the most egregious example. That's all anyone seemed to do, take what they could from him, whether it was borrowed from his fame to make their own star rise, or to use his presence to bolster their business, or to ask him to donate to their cause. It felt like there wasn't anyone who wanted to actually help him.

Maybe it was just the way he was looking at it. Maybe he was the one who was constantly taking, and other people were giving, and he was looking at it wrong. But the emails that he had just seen weren't instigated by him. They were instigated by others, to use him for what they could gain from him.

A knock at the door had him composing himself, making sure he kept from running to answer it.

He took a breath, checking his mind for any creative glimmer, before he opened the door.

He wasn't sure he had seen her full in the face of the daylight before, and her big blue eyes startled him. Her golden blonde hair was caught back in a ponytail, and she stood with an easy smile on her face, a mop in one hand, a sweeper in the other.

"Hello. Are you ready for your weekly cleaning?" she asked, tilting her head and somehow infusing humor into those benign words.

She's fine, she's funny, she's brightness in my day.

The words came on the melody of their own as he stood staring at her.

Amazing.

Her face started to change, and he realized that he had been just standing there staring at her.

"Of course. Please come in. I'm ready."

He stepped back, allowing her to enter, and then realized that she probably had more things to carry. He didn't really want to get into the habit of helping her when she came, but... There just was something in his upbringing that would not allow him to allow her to go out and carry the heavy things in while he sat around.

"I'll go carry the rest of the stuff in."

"You don't have to do that. I know you want to work. So, I'll try to be as efficient as possible. I figured I would clean the living room first, and that way, you can spend the rest of your time in there if you want to, and the kitchen and the bedroom and the bath will take a little bit more time."

She'd obviously thought about it and wanted to try to do what would be the most considerate thing for him. He had been thinking to himself how the people around him were not considerate, always taking from him, and then this woman shows up.

She's different, she brings joy. She's considerate without wanting anything in return.

Another line, fully formed on melody, floated through his head.

He couldn't wait to get back to his notebook to jot it down.

But again, the words in his head seemed to blot out the fact that he was supposed to be having a conversation. He'd never had this problem before, where songs popped into his head, fully formed on melody, while he was in the middle of talking to someone.

"I'll just bring the stuff in and set it down here, and then I'll get out of your way."

"It's me who's trying to stay out of your way," she said with a laugh, shaking her head, but she moved into the house, going immediately to the living room, where she took the blanket that he had out, folded it up, and continued to busy herself while he walked out to grab the rest of her things.

Words floated in his head, music wrapping around them; he could even hear the harmony. Hear the guitar solo. It all fit together so perfectly. He wanted to attach a recorder to his brain, but of course he couldn't do that.

He finished carrying the things in as quickly as he could, then grabbed his notebook and pen where he left it on the counter, and sat on a chair, jotting everything down as best he could.

He wanted his guitar; he wanted to be able to sing.

Maybe he could take it outside. In fact, after he got all the words that had come to him, he grabbed his guitar and went outside.

He probably should have told her what he was doing, but he was too deep in thought, too fixated on the song that seemed to be completely formed. All it needed was a voice.

He hit record on his phone, confident that he was going to nail it the first time, and he was right. All the phrases came together, and even the bridge went down without any trouble or effort on his part.

While it was easy, it still took a little longer than he was expecting, and by the time he had recorded the song from beginning to end, she opened the door with the basket on her hip.

"All finished. I just have to carry my things to the car, and I'm out of here."

He tried to fight back his disappointment. She had inspired him to write what he knew, with the gut feeling that had gotten him where he was, was the best song of his career.

"I'll help you," he said, leaning his guitar against the cabin and setting his notebook on the rocking chair after he stood.

"Really. I do this all the time. For every other house. I promise you, I know that you're being very gentlemanly with lots of manners, but I really can do this."

"I know you can."

He didn't want to explain the urge that not only made him want to help her but the more nebulous urge, the harder to define issue he was having, where he didn't want her to leave. Where she was his muse. Far more than his muse, she was the fire of his creativity.

"All right," she said, lifting a shoulder like there wasn't anything she could do to stop him.

She was dressed similarly to the way she had been before, with yoga pants and a faded T-shirt. The warm weather had held, and the sunshine, bright and cheerful, warmed across the plains.

She waited by her car as he took the last of her things out. He noted that she put his clothes away in drawers and left a dirty clothes basket discreetly in the bathroom, behind the door.

It seemed like everything she had done was geared toward making him comfortable so that his life would be as easy as possible.

She had a true servant's heart.

The idea for a new song popped into his head at that thought. Phrases, disjointed at first, arrived on a melody that was sweet and pure.

"Thanks a lot," she said as he started to step out, barely noticing that he had made it to the car. The song was so vivid it was hard to focus on anything else.

"Sure. Anytime," he said, staring at her and trying to figure out how he could get her to not leave. To finish one song in a day was amazing; to be able to get a second one, which he instinctively knew was going to be just as good, if not better, would be awesome. But he was already acting weird. "See you...Friday."

"That's right. I'll text you Thursday evening if I don't have a grocery list from you by then."

"Thanks," he said and realized after she drove away that he hadn't asked her what he had been meaning to. Something about...cooking. Maybe she could show him a few dishes. Or maybe he could hire her to cook for him.

After she disappeared, the song flitted out of his head.

He practically ran to the rocking chair to write it down. Then he grabbed his guitar and sang the couple of lines that he had. He would work on this and have it finished by the next time he saw her. He would force it, if he had to. Because he wasn't going to sit around and wait on some woman's fancy. He couldn't live his life dependent on someone else. In his experience, no one except himself was dependable.

Chapter Five

"All right, hold that last stretch for just a couple more seconds. Feel that relaxing of your muscles. And go ahead and stand up. Great job today. Thanks for spending the morning with me," Priscilla said, then she hit the stop button on her phone and sighed.

She had gotten up before dawn, gone to the farm, mixed up milk replacer and fed the calves, then came back and did her morning stretching and exercise routine. She had filmed it all.

"Can we talk now?" Justin asked from behind her.

"Yes. Thank you so much for being so good."

"I did my homework. I'm just waiting for you to check it," Zaylee said.

"Did you do your reading assignment?"

"Yeah. I answered all the questions. But I didn't do my worksheet. Do I have to?" she asked, wrinkling her nose.

Priscilla was tempted to say that if Zaylee were in school, she would not ask her teacher if she had to do a homework assignment, but instead, she put a hand on her hip and raised her brows.

Zaylee pressed her lips together and put her head down, looking at her mom under her brows.

Priscilla waited, and Zaylee sighed. "All right. I'm sorry."

"All right. If I assign it, you can't question the assignment." She just wanted to remind her daughter. Truly, she might complain about the work her teacher gave her, but she wasn't going to ask her teachers if she had to do it. She was just going to assume that it had to be done. Now, there were times where Zaylee, especially, forgot to do her homework, and Priscilla had taken to asking her about each class separately, because if she did a blanket, "Do you have your homework done for today?" Zaylee was more than likely to say yes, without thinking about whether she actually did or not.

"Let me have five more minutes, and then we'll start math class, okay, Justin?"

He nodded, scribbling furiously, probably trying to get ahead on his work. He hated to be behind and loved having her give him an assignment so he could whip out the paper and show her that he already did it.

They had already done a short Bible lesson, which had been part of her video blog that morning.

After clicking and swiping a few times and putting the unedited video onto her social media accounts, she walked to the sink and downed a glass of water before filling it up half full and taking it over to the table.

Even though her children were now older, experience had taught her that it was better to spill half a glass than a whole one. And accidents could happen at any time.

As she taught math class, working with Justin on his multiplication tables and skip counting, she heard her phone buzzing with notifications. She had forgotten to turn it off. But the sounds made her smile. When she started her video posting that summer, she'd only had a handful of followers. Then, she'd gone up to a few dozen. And then a few hundred.

Possibly by the end of the week, she would have a thousand.

Slow and steady building. Although, she honestly had to say it had been happening faster than she thought it would. She hadn't expected to get a thousand people interested in what she did in her mornings, let alone more. And yet, that seemed to be what was happening.

Somehow people related to a single mom who got up before dawn, no matter what kind of work she did, and then came home to her kids, did Bible study with them, and then did a fifteen-minute stretching and exercise routine before she started homeschooling for the day... People just seemed to be able to relate to that.

She wasn't sure what it was about it. Maybe it seemed idyllic, but she didn't think so. She didn't only show the good stuff. She showed everything, including herself not wanting to get out of bed, forgetting her gloves, getting kicked by a calf, spilling an entire bottle of milk, and all the various places calf poop could land. Places that a normal person had no clue about.

Part of the comments were always about wanting to see more on the farm, and the other half of her comments were about what she ate and what she cooked for her kids. She had been knocking around the idea of doing an afternoon video showing her meal prep time, although she didn't want to make her entire day about taking videos.

It didn't hurt her children to have to be quiet for fifteen minutes while she did her stretching exercises, but she didn't want them constantly being shushed or pushed into a corner so that she could grow her following.

Of course, if the following was going to help support them, then she wanted them to be on board with it. And she would do what she needed to do.

"All right, let's take the speed drill, and then you can work on your homework while Zaylee and I do her math."

It was so tempting to go over and look at her phone, but she managed to teach until it was time for their cookie break before she picked it up.

"Did you get a lot of comments today, Mommy?" Zaylee asked before taking a big bite of an iced sugar cookie. Alaska didn't just make cookies with the kids, she made works of art, and the kids were learning at a very young age to imitate her.

"They really liked our Bible lesson today on how none of the families in the Old Testament were perfect. There was dysfunction everywhere. A lot of people hadn't thought about that before."

"You said they were dysfunctional," Justin said, smirking before he too took a big bite of a cookie.

Crumbs fell all over the place, but Priscilla didn't worry about them. She was so happy to have her children there that the mess really didn't bother her at all. Maybe that was one of the benefits that had happened with her losing them for a time. She appreciated them so much more. Something silly like a mess did not upset her equilibrium like it might have at one point.

Plus, she saw it as a teaching opportunity. If he didn't make such a big mess, there wouldn't be such a big mess for him to clean up when he was finished.

"What did you say?" Zaylee asked, and Priscilla proceeded to read some of the comments and her replies. She answered a few more of them and liked several others. It had become a ritual with her and the kids, and she felt that including the children in this made them feel like they were part of it, so when she asked them to be quiet during the stretching, or she set the camera up so that they could film their Bible time in the morning, the kids knew exactly who was going to be seeing it and understood where the comments came from.

Justin had asked several times for her to get him up before dawn and take him to feed the calves too. She hadn't done that yet. She knew he was more than old enough to do it, but she kind of liked the quiet time for herself in the morning, and she also didn't want her son to start working too much too soon. Some kids really needed to work more than what they did, but on the ranch the way they were, she figured that her son would probably end up working too much, rather than not enough.

Still, she couldn't be unhappy with the direction her life was going. Although, sometimes she did look off into the future and wonder what it would look like ten or twenty years from now when her kids were grown, and she was alone. Would she be as happy?

She certainly hadn't anticipated being by herself when she had gotten married years ago. She thought she and her husband would create a life together, maybe even a similar life to what was happening on the ranch now. Where all of their children were able to stay around, helping in various aspects and being a family together.

God will work that out. You have no idea what's going to happen between now and then.

She didn't want to be afraid of the future. She didn't want to dread it. She wanted to enjoy each day as it came and accept that the future might not be what she wanted, but it would be something she could handle, along with the Lord.

And that was as good as she could promise herself.

Chapter Six

It was Priscilla. There was no doubt about it. That was all Cooper could think as he struggled for the rest of the week to come up with anything other than those few lines that had hit him since he had seen her.

How could he get her to be around more? He didn't want her around so much that they were together all the time, but he wanted to be around her enough to know that he could be inspired to write at least one song a week. That would be more than sufficient. He'd end up with twenty-five songs, and some of them he could just sing, accompanied by his guitar, and put the video on social media. That would give him an income from his social media accounts, which had been completely dead since he had left the spotlight.

Thankfully, it was Friday and she would be showing up with his grocery list. He had sent the list of things that he wanted to her without her having to ask. He looked online a little bit and then just settled on snack food. He was going to need to do something else, and maybe... maybe he could talk to her about it today.

He was standing at the window watching as her car came into view.

His hands started to tingle, and his heart beat faster.

It was because she was his muse and from the excitement that his creativity might be stimulated. He already had the snippet of a song that he had been working on, wrangling with, and trying to wrestle into some semblance of music ready. He had it written down in his notebook and had his guitar leaning against the wall, where it would be easy to grab as soon as she left.

Today, she wouldn't be there as long as she had been on Monday when she'd been cleaning and changing his linens, but hopefully it would be long enough for him to get what he needed.

Part of him felt a little guilty. Like he was using her the way other people used him and it bothered him so much.

Part of him figured it didn't hurt. He wasn't asking her to do anything that she hadn't already volunteered to do and that he was already paying for. The agreement that his publicist had made was that he would stay, they would do his laundry and bring his groceries. The price they quoted had included all of that.

Not so for the cooking.

He took a breath and blew it out. He needed to focus on talking to her. If the creativity came, he would encourage it, welcome it, but he also needed to remember that he had something to say.

He opened the door almost immediately after she knocked, and she looked surprised.

"Hello." She smiled at him, picking up the bags she set down in order to knock on the door. "I hope you had a great week."

"It's been good," he said, although it hadn't been as good as what he wanted. He hadn't gotten anything new written since she'd left last time.

Waiting, watching, hoping. Watching for her to come. Because she brought all the good feelings of creativity with her.

It was happening again. The song, already on a melody, flitting through his head.

He wanted to grasp it, hold onto it, remember it so that he could write it down as soon as she left, but he needed to talk to her.

Still, he had to help as well. He walked outside to grab the rest of the groceries and carry them in, humming the melody to himself, hoping he didn't lose it before she left.

"Thank you," she said as he walked in, setting the groceries on the counter.

"I have a request," he said, not sure how else to broach it and not wanting to preface things with a bunch of small talk.

"All right," she said, seemingly unconcerned that it might be something she couldn't do or wouldn't want to. Totally trusting him as she turned around with a smile, her head tilted to one side, waiting.

"You probably noticed I got a lot of snack food."

"That's the way some people eat, I guess," she said, shrugging her shoulder. He didn't know what she knew about how other people ate. This girl who had been secluded on the North Dakota prairie all her life. She probably didn't know much of anything. If he had stayed in rural Virginia where he had been born, he would be the same, not doing or seeing or knowing anything but where he'd grown up.

He didn't necessarily think that was a bad thing. In fact, he probably knew a little more than what he wanted to and sometimes wished he could go back to his roots.

"It's not really the way I want to eat." He stopped. "It's not the way I can eat." He had a certain image that he needed to present to fans. Not that he wanted to get wrapped up in his image necessarily, but they didn't want to see him unhealthy standing out on stage. Plus, in order to give them the kind of show that they wanted, he needed to stay in shape.

"I see," she said, and he had a feeling that she did. But she was only seeing the one side. The idea that he was concerned about his image. Not that he was concerned about his energy levels and health levels in order to give people the show they wanted. He didn't want to take the time to explain to her.

"I guess I never learned to cook much."

"A lot of people don't," she said, brushing off his concern that she might be judging him for not knowing what he should know as an adult in his mid-thirties.

"I was wondering if...if you might have a few simple meals that you could teach to me. Stuff that's healthy and I could prepare without too much trouble. I guess I have enough time to cook complicated stuff, but I don't want to."

"I totally get it. Some people love cooking, love the relaxation of creating delicious food, and some people just want to get the necessary evil out of the way as painlessly and quickly as possible."

"I'm in the second group," he said, his eyes narrowed a bit.

She chuckled at him. "I used to be too. I think I shifted more to being in the first group, but it has to do with cooking for my children and not so much for me. Or maybe it has to do with just enjoying life. Moment by moment. Because each moment is what makes a life, isn't it?"

"I suppose so."

"And enjoying what you do, enjoying those moments, is key to enjoying your life. At least, that's what I've learned anyway."

"Interesting," he said. He hadn't really thought about that. He knew he couldn't continue to harbor the bitterness and the anger and the negativity that he'd had since Regina Blue, but he also hadn't thought that each moment he didn't enjoy was one moment of his life gone.

She looked at him expectantly, and he realized another phrase was running through his head. It didn't feel like the same song though. It felt like a different one.

"Would you be interested?" he asked, not really wanting to get rid of her but wanting to have a moment to write a few things down.

"Sure. I think I'd like to do it at my place, if that's okay. I'm actually trying out a few new recipes myself this week. I..." She closed her mouth.

"What?" he asked, wondering if she had a husband or boyfriend or someone that would be upset if he were hanging around. "I would pay you. I'm not asking you to hang out with me because you like me, so if you're afraid that I'm going to mess up a relationship that you already have, you can put your mind at rest."

"No. Nothing like that. I just have a vlog I've been doing in the morning, and I was thinking about adding cooking onto it. That's kind of what I was thinking when I got the ingredients for the new food."

"I see. Well, I don't want any part of that," he said, meaning that with every bone in his body. He didn't want to have anything to do with any kind of social media presence. He wanted to be completely hidden.

"I know. That's why I wanted to say something to you. I understand that that's not interesting to you. But... We'll just have to work it out. So that you're not there on the days that I'm recording. That's all."

"That's fine. You know my schedule is not exactly booked solid, so if you tell me what days will work for you, I can make them fit."

"Well, tonight and tomorrow should be fine, although we do have dude ranch guests. I'm not sure my help is that required for them, though. Sunday it will be, and we'll be going to church in the morning anyway." She paused, and then she looked at him. "You're welcome to come to church with us on Sunday or to eat Sunday dinner with us if you'd like. I mean, you're always welcome."

He nodded curtly and brushed it off. He didn't want them to start to expect him. "Maybe someday, but right now, that's a no."

"I get it." She nodded. "Monday I'm here, Tuesday I should be free, and Wednesday and Thursday were the days I was thinking that I would do the video."

"All right. So, it looks like tomorrow would be a good day, or maybe Tuesday."

"Yeah. Either works for me."

"Let's do tomorrow. What time are you thinking?"

"I usually start supper around four. Typically my kids are off playing with their cousins, and if I've gone to help at the farm, I'm done."

"I see. You work on the farm too?" He didn't mean to ask that personal question. It just came out because he was surprised.

"Yes."

She didn't elaborate, and he didn't ask anything more. He was still humming a tune in his head, and there was a big part of him that wanted her to leave quickly.

"I'll just throw the rest of these vegetables in the refrigerator and leave the other things out for you to put away?" she asked, when she figured out that he wasn't going to say anything more.

"Yeah. That sounds good."

There wasn't that much to put in the refrigerator, and she bade him goodbye as she walked to the door.

"I'll see you at your house at four tomorrow," he said.

She nodded. "I'll expect you."

The door hadn't clicked closed before he grabbed his guitar and sat down on a stool, jotting down some words, then pushing record on the phone.

He worked it out, adjusted some lines to go with the other lines that he had, and he was pretty sure that the song was going to be a good one. Even better than the one he'd written last week.

There was a part of him that wanted to share it with the world now, but part of being successful was being patient. Waiting until the right time to share, and he would do that.

And then, a thought struck him.

If she was trying to build a social media presence, he could probably search for her and find out exactly what she was doing.

It had surprised him to hear that she was working on the farm. What did she do, drive a tractor around? She just didn't seem like that kind of girl. But he could kinda see that turning into a song too.

Without giving himself any time to talk himself out of it, he swiped to a social media site and put her name in. Priscilla was not a common name, and as he figured, it wasn't hard to find an account that belonged to her. She had a straightforward picture of her face, and it wasn't in some kind of sexy pose with her lips pursed, or her eyes darkly shadowed and batting at the camera. She just looked like a fresh, sweet girl. So middle America.

She would fit his brands perfectly, he thought to himself before he sat up straight. No. He did not want to think like that. She was not becoming part of his brand.

She was just perfect because she inspired him to write songs. That was all.

He looked at her latest video, which was her getting up in the morning and feeding calves, and then as he watched, she came back and got her kids out of bed, sitting down at the table and doing a Bible lesson with them. And then, she ended it with some stretching exercises.

Nothing too glamorous, nothing earthshaking. Her following was small, barely a thousand people.

Compared to his millions of followers, she was small potatoes.

Well, he didn't have anything to worry about from her. She wasn't going to be videotaping him, and she definitely wasn't going to be using him to further her own interests. But he bookmarked the site. Perhaps she did have in her head that she could build her following based on his fame.

She hadn't mentioned him at all, but just because someone didn't mention it didn't mean that they weren't planning on it. He'd learned that lesson all too well.

Was he a little bitter? Was he being a little judgmental? Judging Priscilla based on what Regina Blue had done?

Perhaps. Perhaps he was. But he felt like his past experience had encouraged him to do that, and it wasn't necessarily a bad thing. He was just being realistic. Right?

Chapter Seven

"He did what?" Ada said, holding her plate in her hand and staring at Priscilla.

Ada was the closest sibling in age to Priscilla, after her twin sister Phoebe. She loved her twin, but her twin was happily married, which made Priscilla extremely happy, of course. But sometimes it was hard to handle, since her own marriage had ended in such disaster.

It wasn't that she didn't enjoy seeing her twin happy, because she did. It was just... Sometimes she couldn't relate, and she knew her twin couldn't relate to her.

But Ada, who had never married, didn't make Priscilla feel uncomfortable or jealous. That was the bottom line. Sometimes she was jealous of her twin's happy marriage. Not that she was jealous in a bad way. She didn't wish any ill on Phoebe at all. It was just... She wished that had been the way her own marriage had turned out, and she was still kind of clueless as to why it hadn't. Was there something she could have done to change it?

But as many times as she'd gone over everything that she'd done, she'd never been able to figure out something that she could have done differently that would have kept all the bad things from happening. The only thing she could think of was to have not married her ex, but she didn't have any signs that she should have known that. She'd thought God was okay with it, her brothers were on board, and no one had anything bad to say about him.

It would have been different if she would have defied everyone and insisted on her own way, and then she would feel like she was getting her just desserts. And she would know what not to do if there was ever a next time.

But that wasn't the way it had gone at all.

She realized Ada was still waiting on an answer. "He asked me if I would teach him how to cook, basically."

"Oh my goodness. Do you realize how many views your blog would get if people found out that Cooper Cordray was on with you? Your views would go through the stratosphere!"

Priscilla was happy that Ada was happy for her, but she got it all wrong. "No. It's not like that. He was very clear that he didn't want to be on camera at all. I felt like I had to tell him that I was doing the vlog, just because I know that he wants to keep a low profile. And I didn't want him thinking that I was doing something weird on the side."

"You're not doing anything weird on the side. Everybody puts videos on social media nowadays. In fact, it's the weird people who don't."

"Well, our family is weird then."

"You know what I mean," Ada said as they walked through the line. When they had the whole family together, there were so many of them that they could not fit in the farmhouse anymore. So they used the bunkhouse to have family get-togethers and Sunday dinners. Even if they had people staying at the dude ranch, they were on their own for their Sunday meal. Priscilla thought that maybe someday they would have their own church service, but it would mean hiring a preacher or having her brothers preach, and none of them felt qualified.

That was something for down the road, and Priscilla figured God would provide what they needed when they needed it.

She watched as her children played with their cousins, talking and joking and filling their plates and talking to their aunts and uncles and just surrounded by a loving family.

"I don't care how weird our family is. I love it. I am so grateful to our parents that they decided to do the hard thing, rather than the easy thing."

"And have a whole pile of kids?"

"Sure. You know how people look down on that now? How much grief they got, how hard it is to try to follow all the state regulations, when you have more than two or three children."

"Two point five, right?"

"I think it's gone down some. I think it's like down to one point nine or something like that."

"Wow. Yeah, small families are really missing out."

Priscilla took a scoop of the broccoli that she'd steamed just a few minutes ago and set it on a plate. "But there are advantages to small families too."

"I don't disagree with you. Parents can afford to do a lot more for and with their kids. We never traveled or went anywhere. Can you imagine buying airplane tickets for fourteen people?"

"I don't even think you're allowed to buy that many airplane tickets at one time."

"I'll have to take your word on that, because I've never tried to, but yeah. So some of us have never flown on an airplane. That's me," Ada said with a grin.

"Does it bother you?" Priscilla asked. Because it never had bothered her. That she hadn't done what everyone else in the world had done.

"No. Doesn't bother me at all. I mean, I guess I would like to travel. I guess I do wonder sometimes what Disneyland is like. Or what would it be like to just get in a car and have the entire family right there."

"Yeah. We never even had that."

"Right? We always had an SUV, and before that, we had the 15-passenger van."

"And it was full!"

They laughed together. Coming to the end of the line, they went and sat down at the end of one of the tables.

"But I guess I just felt like we had so much more. All of this," Ada said, throwing a hand around and indicating the entire room full of laughing, happy people.

"Not that we didn't have our share of fights and arguments,"

Priscilla said. "But I have to agree with you. I mean, can you imagine how quiet it would be to have a mom and dad and two kids and that would be it in the house?"

"Yeah. I mean, no wonder kids go to school. There'd be no one to play with. You'd have to go outside and find friends, and if you lived in a place like this where there were no houses nearby, you'd have to learn to...play by yourself."

"Yeah. Or watch TV all the time," Priscilla said, understanding why some kids got addicted to those kinds of things. She supposed that the idea of not having anyone else to play with was hard.

"We had so much fun homeschooling. I mean all of us together, it just... I don't know. I can see positives on both sides. There are definitely negatives on both sides, but I'm not unhappy with the way my life turned out. I don't regret the things that we couldn't do as a family because we were too big or didn't have enough money. I think the love and laughter and support and happiness that we had together far outweighed that."

"And I could see how someone from a smaller family might have thought that a lack of money might have made things worse. If they hadn't been able to take their ski trips in Aspen, or vacations to Disney World, or flying here or there."

"I don't know how we got on that subject, because you were telling me about Cooper Cordray. The Cooper Cordray who is going to be at your house cooking." She shook her head. "How cool is that?"

"All right. I have to admit, I'm a little bit awestruck, but he doesn't act like you think a superstar would act, you know?"

"In what way?" Ada said, like she couldn't understand.

Priscilla watched her kids, laughing and talking, as she thought. "I guess I just thought he would be kind of like a stage presence, you know? Catering to the crowd and smiling and taking requests and... I don't know. He's just very quiet. He usually seems very preoccupied, and he doesn't have the slightest bit of interest in doing anything with the family."

"I can understand why. I guess it's kind of like you, when your ex left, and the divorce hit, and it was all so hard. You just felt like you needed to take shelter somewhere."

"Yeah. That's exactly it. Like I needed to lick my wounds, like a dog going under the porch and resting for a bit."

"You can understand that about him."

"Yes. You're absolutely right. That's exactly how it feels like. But then he asked me to teach him to cook. It seems like if he wanted to be left alone, he would ask me to deliver meals or something. You know?"

"Maybe he didn't realize that was an option." They laughed together.

"Maybe I should offer that to him. Because it is a little disconcerting to think of the guy standing in my kitchen watching me." There was something about him that put her a little on edge. Not necessarily in a bad way, just in a way where she was very aware of his presence. She did like his understated personality and his insistence on being courteous, carrying groceries, carrying her cleaning supplies, and treating her with respect. She definitely liked that. But she figured that was more of his upbringing than his personality.

"You believe all the rumors about him?" she finally asked after they had eaten for a little bit in silence.

"That he got caught trying to steal the songs from that girl who was touring with him?"

"Yeah. I guess that was the gist of it. She claimed that she wrote the songs while she was touring with him, and he claimed that he wrote the songs and she stole the ideas from him."

There had been a big blowup about it, and several venues, which had been sold out, had to refund tickets to the purchasers. The woman who'd been with him had offered to rebook with only her on the billing, but Cooper hadn't even done that. He just disappeared.

"He does seem guilty, but I guess after the experience that I've had with my divorce, I know that there are two sides to every story, and the judge was very quick to believe the slick lawyer that my ex hired, and he didn't really give me any credit at all. I can see how one person can be very convincing."

"You know, at the time, I wondered if anything good could come out of that. You know how the Bible says that God works everything for good, and I just used to sit there and think 'how can He?'"

"I would wonder that too. But you're right. Now that I have a few years between here and there, the pain was great, especially the pain with not getting the kids, not being able to see them, having the judge declare that I didn't get custody, and that my visits were limited." She felt a pang even now thinking about it. "But it definitely changed me. And I think mostly in good ways. Maybe I have some trust issues left over."

"I can totally understand how you'd have trust issues. None of us saw that coming."

"Me least of all," she said, knowing that was absolutely true. "But beyond that, I really do think it's true. God does work all things out for our good. We just have to let Him."

"I think there are some people who would say, how could He work divorce for anyone's good? How could divorce be a part of God's plan?"

"I don't think it is a part of His plan. He's very clear that He hates divorce. He's very clear that He doesn't want that. But He can take anything, even a sin like that, and work it out for good. Because it wasn't like I wanted a divorce. Even after my husband cheated, I would have taken him back just to keep our family together. But he wouldn't. And should I be punished for that? I guess I feel like God says no."

"I agree," Ada said softly.

They ate for a while without talking, and Priscilla wondered, as she always did when she was around Ada, if she would ever get married. There was no point asking her, because Ada would just say that God hadn't brought the right man around yet. And as much as Priscilla would love to see her settled with someone who valued her for who she was, she knew there was no rushing things.

"Do you think you'll ever get married again?" Ada finally asked.

It was funny, since she was resisting asking whether Ada thought she'd ever get married, but Ada didn't seem to hesitate to ask her. But she knew her answer. It was easy.

"No. I don't want to. I feel like I had a chance, and it blew up. And I had no idea that was coming. Why would I want to do that to myself again?"

"I can see how that would be a problem. After all, no one saw that your ex would cheat on you. And there's no guarantee that the next guy wouldn't be just as wonderful, with all the great credentials, and end up doing the same thing."

"Exactly."

"But I guess I could say the same thing. Maybe I just shouldn't get married, because I can't be guaranteed that whoever I choose isn't going to cheat."

When Ada said it like that, it sounded a little different. After all, she wanted Ada to be happy and not to be afraid to step out in marriage, just because she was afraid her husband was going to cheat.

"I guess you know that that doesn't sit very well."

Ada grinned. "Any more than you saying you'll never get married again because of the same reason."

Priscilla nodded, understanding the lesson Ada was trying to impart. She understood it, but it didn't mean that she was going to apply it.

Chapter Eight

Cooper hit send and thought about what an idiot he was. He had no idea where Priscilla lived. He knew the direction her car came every time she came, and he thought that she had mentioned living in a cabin, but he could have been wrong about that. Man, he was supposed to be at her house in three minutes, and he didn't even know which one was hers. And it hadn't occurred to him until just then that he didn't.

Great. Now he was going to have to deal with kids.

It wasn't that he didn't like kids. He had an older brother and older sister, and they were married with some children, and he saw them occasionally, but he supposed he'd always been wrapped up in himself and his own problems, and he never really paid much attention to the kids.

What did that say about him?

Growing up, there had been kids in the neighborhood who would come around, some of them younger, and it always seemed like the younger ones were the ones who wanted to tattle and cry over everything.

Somehow he got it in his head that he didn't really like kids, and he wasn't sure where that idea had come from. Maybe society had foisted it on him. Because society didn't really seem to value children. It certainly didn't encourage families to have a lot of them.

He remembered his grandma telling stories about growing up in a big family. Apparently the family who owned this ranch was a large family as well.

Okay. I'll watch for them.

He sent that back and glanced at his guitar, leaning against the wall by his notebook which was on the table.

He hated leaving that and wondered if he would be as inspired to write at her house as he was when she walked into his.

It was intriguing the way she sparked thoughts, when his mind was as dry as a desert when she wasn't around.

Before long, he saw the two kids coming over the rise, and he walked out his front door, feeling the chill in the air and walking back in to grab a long-sleeved button-down.

He fit in around here with it, and it was the kind of clothes he was comfortable in.

Maybe at some point he would be interested in walking around the ranch and getting to know and see some of the things that went on. He'd been here long enough, nearly two weeks, that he was starting to get a little bit antsy.

Or maybe that was just because his creativity was at a zero, unless Priscilla was in his house. And then, it was bubbling over so fast he could hardly write fast enough to get it all written down before it left him.

"Are you Mr. Cooper?" the little boy said. He must've been ten or eleven years old. He walked like he knew where he was going and had purpose.

"I am. You must be my guide."

"I'm Justin," the kid said, sticking out his hand.

"Nice to meet you, Justin," he said, a little surprised that the kid was so forward. Not that it was off-putting. It was actually kind of intriguing. Like someone had worked with him on it, and he had taken it all in.

"I'm Zaylee," the little girl said, but she didn't stick out her hand.

"It's nice to meet you both. I take it Miss Priscilla is your mom?"

They nodded.

"You're supposed to follow us, and we're gonna show you where we live. Mom said you were safe," the little boy announced before he turned around, and they started walking back the direction they'd come.

Their mom said he was safe. How did she know?

Maybe they had been instructed not to talk to strangers, although if his understanding was correct, they had strangers coming in and out all the time on the ranch. Maybe they just weren't allowed to be alone with them or something.

He thought about the kid's comment and then dismissed it, figuring that whatever it was, it wasn't personal to him.

"So your mom's a pretty good cook?" he asked, figuring that he had actually hired her to teach him how to cook, and he didn't even know. He just made an assumption, which could have been completely and totally wrong.

"She makes good food. She has a social media account, and she has a thousand followers," Justin said, and Cooper pretended to be impressed.

"A whole thousand? Wow. That's a lot."

"She says it's growing every day. We help her with it sometimes." Zaylee was cute, and she spoke matter-of-factly, like there was nothing to hide.

He supposed there wasn't. Although, with his new knowledge of people, he had a tendency to want to pull away from them, hide what he was doing, to not let anyone know, so they could not sabotage it. It wasn't a good way to live, but if he wanted to protect himself, it was what he needed to do.

"What do you do?" Justin asked, like they'd talked about their blog, so now it was his turn.

"Well, I grew up in Virginia. On a place very similar to this. Only smaller." Smaller was an understatement. It hadn't been anything compared to this. It had been a small farm in the backwoods of Virginia that had been hard-pressed to do more than eek out enough of a living for his grandma to raise him and his two older siblings. It had been hard work, and when he left the farm, he vowed he would never go back.

Interesting that now he kind of missed it.

"But what do you do now?" Justin asked again.

"Nobody's told you?" he asked, unable to believe that someone with the name the size of his would have been able to come here, and not one of the adults had said anything within hearing of the children of who they knew he was.

"My cousin said you were a singer, but she says she doesn't like you anymore. Is that really what you do?"

There. He didn't think that it was possible for him to be here and for people to not know who he was. Maybe he was right to try to stay to himself.

"That's true. I guess there aren't a whole lot of people who can make a living writing songs and singing them, but I seem to be one of those who was blessed that way."

He stumbled a bit over the word "blessed." He believed in God. He still did, even though he was a little bit angry at the Lord for allowing things to work out the way they had. If God were really just, wouldn't the correct person have been punished? Wouldn't the world have found out that Regina Blue stole his songs and was even now making money on them?

But since God wasn't just, since the world wasn't perfect, since God apparently didn't care about doing right, Regina Blue was getting away with it, and he was holed up here in this godforsaken place, going to spend the winter in the frozen Arctic wilderness.

Okay, maybe he was being a little bit dramatic, but he did feel like God had not done him right.

"Mom has a nice voice, but I don't really like to sing. I mean, sometimes I do it and I don't mind it, but I can't imagine doing that every day. I'd rather be outside." Justin almost sounded like a little man, the way he spoke with such maturity.

It intrigued Cooper, since he thought of kids as being smart-alecky, disrespectful, and rude. But both of these were rather respectful and mature for their age, not that he knew that much about kids. He just wasn't expecting this out of them.

"The big cabin is ours," Justin said, pointing. There were several other smaller cabins in the distance, but the larger cabin was the closest.

That was easy. The closest cabin to his was Priscilla's cabin. They'd been walking less than five minutes, and he figured that he wouldn't have a problem finding it again by himself.

"Mom told us that even though the cabins aren't very far apart, if we get a snowstorm, we're not supposed to go out and try to find your cabin in it. She said we might get lost, and sometimes people who get lost in snowstorms die."

That sounded kind of harsh, but he could see how it would happen. There weren't a lot of landmarks around. And when it was snowing, a person couldn't see very far.

"I'll keep that in mind too. I hope you guys stay safe." He wasn't sure what else to say. That seemed kind of heavy for a young kid, but sometimes those kinds of things saved their lives.

"Mom said she'd be waiting for you inside."

"Aren't you guys coming?"

"She said we could help if we wanted to, but we want to go play with our cousins."

"Your cousins?" he asked, wondering if Priscilla had family around.

"Yeah. All of our cousins live on the farm. There are lots of them." Justin shrugged like it wasn't a big deal.

"This is your family's ranch?" Cooper asked the only question that seemed to make sense. He'd known the ranch was owned by a family, but he hadn't realized that Priscilla was part of that family. He'd thought she was a hired worker.

"Yeah. Everybody owns it. But Uncle Ezra is usually the one who is pretty much in charge. Him and Uncle Tobias. Mom says we're lucky to have such a big family."

"How many people are in the family?" he asked, wondering what a big family was. Five kids? Six?

"I think there's like eight or ten?" Justin scrunched his nose up. And started naming off people.

When he was done, Zaylee reminded him of a couple names that he missed.

"Oh. Yeah."

"And Mom too," Zaylee said.

Cooper tried to fight back a laugh. Of course their mom was included in that.

"I think twelve," he said.

"Wow. Twelve."

"Yeah. They said that not a lot of people have a family like that, so we should be pretty happy."

"All right then," Cooper said, wondering what kind of parents would be so insane as to have twelve kids. Even if they had been divorced and remarried and brought their kids from prior marriages, it was a lot.

He watched the kids run off, then he stepped up on the porch and knocked on the door.

He waited a couple of seconds until Priscilla opened it, looking adorable with an apron tied around her waist. He couldn't remember the last time he'd seen a woman in an apron who wasn't a waitress.

Immediately song lyrics began forming in his head, and a song, total and complete, seemed to march through his consciousness.

He had never had songs come completely formed in his head like that, with the melody and everything.

He tried to shake it off. Even though it seemed like a really great song, he had told himself that he wasn't going to do that this time. Although, the idea of spending more time with Priscilla so he could write more songs had been in the back of his mind when he asked about her teaching him how to cook. He hadn't even known whether she could cook or not. So he must have had ulterior motives. But he didn't want to be that kind of person, because that made him no better, actually worse, than Regina Blue.

"Hey. Sorry I didn't give you directions before. I couldn't believe it when you sent me that text." She pulled the door back and indicated for him to come in.

Her cabin was slightly bigger than his, which made sense, since he could tell by looking at it that it was larger.

"I appreciate you having me. And I should have asked."

If she noticed that he didn't know for sure whether she could cook or not when he asked for lessons, she didn't mention it.

"No. The responsibility lay on my shoulders. But you're here now, and I'm sure you saw it's not hard to find."

"No. But I could see how you wouldn't want to say it was the first cabin you come to, because I might have struck out in the wrong direction."

"Yes. I could have said it was the first cabin you come to in the direction I always go, but I didn't know for sure that you ever actually watched me go. So, there was that too."

"Well, anyway, it was kind of you to send your children. Although they seemed eager to go play with their cousins."

"It's always nice when they're done with their school for the day and they can take off and do something on the ranch. I am blessed to be surrounded by a lot of family."

"Are there really twelve siblings?" he asked, holding his breath and wondering if the kids were actually right.

"How did you know?" she asked, walking over to the counter and pointing to a black apron. "You can wear that if you'd like. I wasn't sure how you felt about your clothes."

"I have someone who washes them for me, so I guess I'm not super picky about them."

"I'll have to put a bug in her ear that she might be getting things that are slightly dirtier than usual," she said.

"I'm going to try to stay clean," he said. "Without the apron."

"It's your choice. I just figured I'd offer it in case you wanted it. And in case I didn't answer your question adequately, yes. I have eleven siblings, out of the same parents. I lost my parents when I was young, and my youngest sister, Lois, was barely two. So, my parents aren't even around for you to ask them what in the world they were thinking."

He laughed, figuring she must have had people think the exact same things that he had thought, since she seemed ready with answers.

"I should have sent you a text asking what you like to eat. But I know that you don't want to be bothered, so I just made some assumptions."

"All right." He felt a little cautious. What kind of assumptions had she made?

"I assumed that you were not a vegetarian."

"I'm not."

"And I also assumed that when you said you were able to cook a little, you meant that you really couldn't do anything beyond boiling water and perhaps cooking eggs."

"I can do scrambled eggs. That's pretty much it."

"All right then. We're going to start with hamburgers today."

"That's my kind of meal," he said, thinking that she really did have him pegged well.

"Awesome. Then I guessed correctly. Hamburgers are also very easy to make, although the hardest thing is making sure you get them cooked the whole way through. If you like yours rare, I think it'll make today a little bit easier."

"No way. No pink. No blood. It has to be cooked the whole way through, otherwise I won't eat it."

"Gotcha."

She didn't mention how she liked hers, and before Cooper thought about it too much, he asked, "What about you?"

She gave him an eyeball before she said, cautiously, "I like mine bleeding, bloodied, still moving if possible."

"That's so gross!"

"I know, right? And when it's cooked the whole way through, I don't really care for them. Hamburgers are not my favorite anyway, and cooked hamburger is not the slightest bit interesting to me."

"Wow. That's...sad."

"I know." She laughed like she'd been teased about it a lot.

He didn't say anything more, and she went to the refrigerator and got out a package of meat.

"We have our own hamburger here on the ranch, but I bought a package from the store. You hadn't seemed too interested in doing anything with the ranch and I didn't want to use a package of hamburger that you wouldn't recognize from my freezer, so when it's your turn to cook by yourself, you will be lost."

"Okay." He felt like he could have recognized hamburger, but he appreciated the fact that she was trying to make this as easy as possible for him.

"So, this is a one-pound package of burger. You could probably make four hamburgers out of it. I think the hamburgers will be kind of small, although the less fat you have in your burger, the larger it will be when it's done cooking. Since the fat mostly melts out during cooking."

"I got it. Lean meat equals more patties."

"Exactly. Except for people like me, who don't cook it a whole lot, and then fat doesn't melt out. So, I guess technically you're healthier than I am."

She gave him a smile, like it didn't bother her at all if he was the healthier of the two of them. Looking at her figure though and remembering that she had done exercises in the morning on video to post to her socials, he figured that she probably was acutely aware of what was healthy and what was not. For himself, he tried to keep a tab on those things too.

She showed him how to divide the meat into quarters, which was not difficult. It was simple math. And then she showed him how to shape it into patties.

"Now, I wasn't sure how complicated to get. And I think I ought to keep things simple. But typically when I make hamburger, I mix it with different things to give it some flavor and a better texture."

"Okay." He paused, and then he wasn't sure he should ask but said anyway, "What different things?"

"Well, I used to use crackers, but now I mostly use oatmeal. You can put salt and pepper in it, cheese, pretty much anything that you enjoy in your hamburger that doesn't need to be cooked. For example, I wouldn't put mushrooms in with the hamburger. If I wanted mushrooms on my hamburger, I'd cook them separately."

"I don't care for mushrooms."

"All right then. And that would work, if you were eating with someone who likes mushrooms. If you do them separately, people get to choose what they put on. For now, I figured I'd just do the traditional

American burger, with American cheese, onions, tomatoes, and lettuce. Along with a soft roll. Some of my brothers like hard rolls, but I don't care for them."

"Soft rolls are good," he said, thinking that they finally found something they had in common.

Maybe she figured the same, because she smiled at that.

"All right, so, not to make this too complicated, because there's only five ingredients unless you count salt and pepper."

"Which we're not counting?"

"You have salt and pepper shakers on your counter, right?"

He lifted a shoulder. "I think?"

"I'll make sure you do. But I'm almost positive they're there. Yes, I remember moving them when I cleaned on Monday."

"All right. I'll take your word for it."

"All right. So, we have onions and tomatoes. Tomatoes are not really supposed to be put in the refrigerator, and in the winter, I don't, but in the summer, it gets pretty hot and sometimes I do it."

She pointed to the tomatoes that sat on the counter beside an onion and then went to the refrigerator and pulled out some lettuce.

"So you're telling me that I need to order these things when I order my groceries."

"That's right. If you want to make burgers, and you want to have these things on them, you need to make sure you order them."

"I know that's common sense, but I'm not used to having to worry about ingredients. I just tell somebody what I want and..." He realized how entitled it sounded, and while her face did not seem to change, it was almost like a microexpression went across it that made him realize that what he was saying was completely unknown to her. "Sorry. I grew up poor, but my grandma never made us learn to cook."

"My mom taught me. I remember cooking with her a lot before she died. And then, once she and Dad... Anyway, I did a lot of cooking. Because there were a lot of us, and someone needed to."

"So no one stepped forward to take care of you guys?"

"Do you know any crazy people who would take care of twelve kids?"

"But the older kids...were adults?"

"Yeah. I'm actually the second oldest. My brother Ezra is the oldest. And then I have a twin sister, who is a few minutes younger than I am. And then there were two boys before my next sister. The guys mostly took care of the farm, and the girls tended to things in the house. But we all helped with everything, if that makes sense."

"So in other words, nobody had assigned roles, you just did what you are good at."

"That's right." She nodded, and then she pointed to the onion and the lettuce. "Would you like to cut one up?"

"I can do the onion," he said, thinking about how he liked big thick slices of onion on his hamburger.

"All right. I'll do the lettuce. I usually rinse it off with water, but I don't get too excited about it. Just make sure you get all the dirt and bugs off."

"There are bugs on lettuce that you get from the store?"

"Not usually, but just in case there are. Plus, it would probably be better if you had bugs than the spray they put on to keep the bugs off, but that's just me."

He hadn't thought of that, but she was probably right. He was a lot more grossed out by the bugs, but the spray was probably a lot worse for him.

She seemed like she had so much common sense, and he really enjoyed talking with her. His head was buzzing with melodies and song lyrics, but he tried to put that all aside. He could hardly write anything down when he hadn't brought his pen and notebook.

"I like to get all the toppings ready first, because to me, burgers are best when they're hot. So you want to cook the burger last. But some people put the burgers in the pan and then prep the toppings while they're cooking. If I'm in a rush, I might do it that way, but I have to be fast. And I didn't want to rush today."

"Would I be too much of a dork if I asked you if we could write this down?"

"I don't think so. It's a lot to take in, if you've never done it before."

She didn't seem like she was judging him at all, but this had to be simple for her, and he was acting like it was some kind of major difficult thing.

"I'll tell you what. After we're done with this, I'll text you everything we did, okay?"

She did not act like it was an issue or that he was being childish about it, which he kind of felt like he was.

"Thank you. I would appreciate it."

"My pleasure. Here's a knife for you. Be careful, I like to keep my knives very sharp."

"I've used knives before," he said, feeling like he needed to say that, because he felt more like a child than ever. Her own children had said sometimes they cooked with their mother, and here he was, an adult who needed help making hamburgers.

"So, I just pull leaves off the lettuce, and it's kind of hard to only cut part of a tomato, so I usually slice the whole thing. If there are any slices left over, you can put them in a baggie and stick them in the fridge to go along with any leftover hamburgers. But usually one tomato is good for four burgers."

"Got it," he said, and maybe he turned his head just a little or lost his concentration for just a second, but the next thing he knew, he had sliced through his middle finger on his left hand, and it started bleeding profusely.

He dropped the knife and said, "Ouch!" He had a couple of other words that he almost said, but he swallowed them back just in time.

"Oh goodness," Priscilla said, setting her knife down and hurrying to the paper towels she had sitting by the sink.

She was back in a couple of seconds with the paper towel folded enough to make a bit of a compress, which she put on the cut and squeezed.

"That actually looks like a deep cut. Once we get the blood stopped, we'll take another look, but on first glance, it looks like something that I would take my kids to get stitched over."

"I'm not going to get stitches," he said.

"Let's wait and see. My rule of thumb is, if it stops bleeding on its own, then no stitches. But if it doesn't, then we go for stitches."

"That's a good rule of thumb for your kids," he said. But he wasn't going to the hospital. He could just imagine how the paparazzi would be, and he didn't want to deal with that, over something as stupid as him cutting himself with a kitchen knife. It would be all through the news that Priscilla had tried to stab him after he'd accosted her or something.

She gave him a look, but she didn't argue with him. She couldn't possibly understand what his life was like, and he didn't want to have to explain it to her now.

But then, he remembered how patient she had been explaining everything that he needed to know with the hamburgers. She hadn't held anything back, and she hadn't not explained it because it was too much trouble.

"I'm sorry. I know I was kinda short about the whole hospital thing. I... I just feel like the paparazzi will be there, and they'll make up a whole story about how I tried to attack you and say you had to stab me or something like that. Then there will be a big blowup, and I'll have to deal with it." His voice was subdued as he stared, almost unseeing, at his hand.

At where she had her fingers wrapped around his, putting a good bit of pressure.

"It's okay. I guess... That's not the world I live in, and I didn't even think about that. I'm sorry."

"I don't expect you to understand. Someone who hasn't been there really couldn't. It's...a whole different world."

She nodded, and he had the feeling that she didn't have to be there in order to get that he would hate that.

But she didn't say anything else.

"Let's take a look at it," he said.

She laughed. "You're worse than the kids. Sometimes it just takes a little bit of time for your platelets to get things clotted up. Give it a bit."

He tried not to be impatient, but he didn't like to just stand there with her holding his finger. It gave him too much time to think.

"I'm going to delay supper," he finally said.

"I was just thinking that you're going to have a hard time playing your guitar once we wrap this thing up. Whether you get stitches, or whether you don't."

"Man, I never even thought about that." What was he going to do if he was stuck in the cabin without being able to make music? He would go stir-crazy pacing from one side of it to the other.

"If you're not able to play for a bit, it might be a good time for you to come out and see the ranch. The kids would be happy to take you around, or you're welcome to just wander around yourself. We get that a good bit with the dude ranch people. But I think everyone knows you're staying here."

"The kids said they knew I was a singer."

"I think it was Mina that recognized your name. She's old enough to have been into your music."

She didn't say anything more, and her gaze dropped to his hand. It made him feel like maybe Mina had said something about why he wasn't making music anymore or why he was hiding out.

He wanted to jump her about it, to ask, but he also really didn't want to know. If her opinion of him had already been compromised, there wasn't anything he could do about it, and maybe it was just best if he worked from a position of ignorance.

"All right, I think maybe we can peek at it now," she said, after a few moments of silence, where he couldn't think of anything to say. For some reason, the idea that she had heard the story and believed Regina Blue bothered him more than he wanted to admit.

She carefully lifted the paper towel, which stuck a little bit to his hand, but not as much as he was afraid it would have. In his experience, tissues were terrible, and he understood why Priscilla had made the effort to get the paper towel.

"It's still seeping," she murmured.

"No stitches," he murmured back.

"Understood," she murmured in reply.

He smiled. He liked her sense of humor. She made him laugh, but not in a goofy, little girl kind of way. She was definitely mature, yet her maturity had not turned her into a humorless stick-in-the-mud.

He supposed he was used to women who were very particular about things and did not like to have their opinions questioned.

Priscilla seemed to be able to go with the flow and did not get upset when he didn't agree with her. Even though she probably had a lot more experience than he did in whether or not something needed stitches.

"All right. If it's okay with you, I'm going to ask you to hold this on tight to see if we can get a little bit more bleeding to stop, and then I'm going to put a bandage on it. I'm going to wrap it kind of snug, hopefully not so snug that we disrupt your circulation, but enough to get it to stop bleeding."

"All right. If possible, I'd like to not lose the finger."

"Then I would recommend you go and get it stitched."

"All right. I get that. So we'll take a chance on losing the finger."

She chuckled again and came back with the box of bandages.

"I was afraid they were going to be pink."

"At one time, they would have been. But these are left from... Anyway." She trailed off awkwardly.

He wanted to press her. They were left from what?

Why was he so interested in that? He should be more concerned about his finger and the fact that he wasn't going to be able to play his guitar for...how long? A week? Two weeks? More?

"I'm going to peel this off, and even if it's still seeping a bit of blood, I'm going to put a bandage on it."

"All right."

"You're sure you don't want to get stitches?" she asked, her eyes on his finger as she pulled the paper towel off, and blood continued to ooze. It wasn't gushing or spurting, but it definitely was seeping.

"Yes. I'm sure." If he was going to die, he would go to the hospital, but he couldn't think of another scenario where he would willingly walk into that type of situation.

"All right then."

She got the bandage out, careful not to touch the bandage part, and he assumed it was because of germs. But she didn't suggest putting any kind of ointment on it. Which he thought was a little bit weird.

"When is the last time you had a tetanus shot?"

"Just a few years ago. I was cut by some stage paraphernalia, and my manager insisted."

"All right. You should be good that way." She pressed the bandage tight and made sure that the ends were sealed. "I would suggest that you take that off when you think it's done bleeding and maybe put a little bit of antibacterial ointment on it. I can give you some, since I assume you probably didn't bring any."

She lifted her eyes, and he shook his head.

"I wouldn't have thought about it either, except I typically do keep a small first aid kit around, since I have children." She lifted a slim shoulder. "But for myself, I wouldn't worry about it."

"Do you think it's going to stop bleeding?"

"Yes. I think eventually it will. The edges are sealed up, and my brothers have had cuts worse than this that have sealed up without stitches. Stitches would probably make it heal faster, but it might actually heal up with less scarring this way."

"All right," he said. Interesting that her brothers had done the same thing. Maybe that was why she wasn't giving him a hard time about it. She'd asked, several times, and let her opinion be known, but she hadn't given him a hard time because he wasn't doing what she wanted. Obviously she'd been in this position before, if her brothers had experienced the same thing. Although, being that they were ranchers, he doubted that they had gotten cut while slicing onions in the kitchen.

It was embarrassing.

"All right. Are you up to finishing our lesson?"

"I am. Although, I don't think I'm going to slice the rest of the onion."

"I think we'll just throw that much away, and I'll slice a little more." She grimaced at the drops of blood that were mixed among the sliced onion.

"Sorry about that."

"Not your fault at all. I just figured you didn't want to eat it too."

"No. You're right. I'm not really into that type of thing."

"Good to know," she said, her voice holding a bit of sarcasm, like she assumed that he wasn't into that type of thing either. "I think if you hold your finger up a little bit or at least set your elbow on the counter and hold your hand up, that will help the bleeding to stop as well."

"I can feel it thumping," he said as he did what she said.

"That's good. Your body will send all the things that it's supposed to to make sure that it heals and kill as many germs as possible. Probably tomorrow is when it will start really hurting."

"Nice. I was just thinking I was being a real trooper with the pain, since there wasn't that much."

"Yeah, you thought you had a high pain tolerance, right?"

He nodded, feeling a little sheepish as she laughed.

"These types of things don't typically hurt until the next day, and then they can really give it to you."

"Thanks for the warning."

"Just speaking from experience. Maybe your experience will be different." She met his eyes, and her smile was easy, her words light, and for the first time in a long time, he felt a little bit of his hard shell slipping away. Maybe he could end up trusting this woman.

No. He'd already learned his lesson there. But it was like he hadn't learned anything, the way he was going.

He tore his eyes away.

She had gathered up the garbage and threw it in the garbage can, washing her hands before she came back and got rid of the sliced onion, slicing a few more rings.

"We were almost done anyway. All that's left to do is to cook the hamburger. I just do that in a skillet on the stove. I know some people who put it in the oven and cook them that way. And I suppose they're just as good."

"Or a grill. They would be good on a grill."

"Yes. They would. I don't have one, and unless you buy one, your cabin doesn't have one either."

"Grilling probably isn't something that you do a lot of in the winter in North Dakota. So I'll probably just let it go."

"You're right. I do know some people who use their grill year-round, because it's a little bit easier than a skillet or the oven, but we'll assume that the people in this room are normal." She gave him a wink, and he found himself laughing.

That was nice. He liked someone to think that he was normal. He hadn't been a superstar for so long that he longed for that exactly, it was just that people didn't really think that of him anymore.

She talked about what she was doing as she did it, telling him what temperature she set the skillet at, and how she covered it, and that she didn't usually push her burgers down because she felt like that pushed the juice out of them, and he listened closely to everything she said. It didn't sound like it was going to be too hard, especially if she gave the written directions, and he would be able to emulate it.

"If you're making cheeseburgers, I always wait until the end to put the cheese on."

"Cheese is important," he murmured.

She nodded, putting the cheese on and then covering it with a lid before moving the skillet off the burner. "My kids are eating at the farmhouse, so if you'd like to eat, we can. Or if you'd like me to send these home with you, I can do that too. I just recommend not putting them in the buns until you're ready to eat them, because the buns get soggy."

"Okay. Noted. That's gross, and I definitely don't want that."

"No. Also, if you enjoy ketchup or mustard, the same applies. My family likes mayonnaise."

"Mayonnaise?" He wrinkled his nose. "That's weird."

"I think we decided that the people in this room are normal."

"Really? I thought we decided that I was."

She laughed. "One of us is distorting reality, I think. I'm not sure which one it is."

He smiled at her, despite the fact that he had just told himself that he wasn't going to trust her, and then he said, "We can eat here if you want. Seems like the burgers would be warmer."

"Yes," she said. "Would you like one or two?"

"I'll take two. I haven't been eating very well over the past week or so, and I'm hungry."

"Alright, two burgers coming right up," she said. There was some clacking and clanging as she got plates and set them on the bar counter, placing them across from each other.

He started to panic a bit. He didn't want to sit and eat with this nice lady. He didn't want to be around this nice lady at all. She was making him forget that he didn't trust people. Plus, he was almost certain that once he got home, he wouldn't be able to at least write out the words to the song that was floating around in his head, and he wouldn't be able to use his guitar to help because of him being ungainly with the knife.

"So here are your two burgers with lettuce, tomato, onion, and I have the ketchup and mustard and mayonnaise here, so you can make your decisions responsibly." She laughed a little. It was impossible for him to not laugh along with her. He wanted to get caught up in her spell, whatever spell she was weaving. She wasn't acting like he was a stranger she barely knew. She was acting like he was...someone she liked just because she liked people and someone she was willing to help.

"You know I owe you. You'll have to tell me what I need to pay you."

"You don't need to pay me. I can't have a man starving to death right beside me, can I?"

She settled on her stool and added, "Would you like to say grace?"

He tried not to swallow his tongue. He grew up saying grace over his food, and he did believe in prayer, but when was the last time he actually said grace?

"You go ahead," he said.

"All right," she said, seeming to not have any reaction to his obvious refusal, and said a short prayer, including a small plea for his finger.

It was like she thought of everything. Was she the most considerate person he'd ever met in his entire life?

Surely not, but there was so much about her that reminded him of his grandmother, reminding him of growing up in Virginia, reminded him of home and family and all the things that had been important to him before he had left it all in order to make a name for himself in music. Not that he had left his roots completely. He still had a moral compass, even if he had crossed it more times than he cared to admit. But he hadn't felt this...feeling of safety and security and of being right where he was supposed to be, comfortable and happy. He didn't know how to explain it.

She's home, where my heart is. She's home, where I want to be.

He resisted the urge to ask for something to write with, trying to push the lyrics away so he could focus on eating. It seemed like when he was around her, the lyrics just came and flowed as easily as water.

"All right. I'll try this mayonnaise thing you claim is so good," he said, picking up the squeezable mayonnaise and putting a liberal amount on his burger.

"You'll become a believer, and you'll never go back," she said warmly before biting into hers.

She sighed and closed her eyes. "This is delicious."

She made it look amazing. He was so hungry, he wasn't sure he was going to even notice the taste, but he needn't have worried. He definitely did, and she was right. The burgers were far superior to anything else he'd eaten for the last two weeks.

"I've got a feeling that mine aren't gonna taste quite this good," he said.

"I think you'll eventually start to make some adjustments, and the ones you cook will be even better, because they'll be geared directly toward your tastes."

She was probably right. If cooking was anything like music, once a person knew the gist of the song, they could add some revision to make it even better. So once he knew the basics of cooking, he could improvise to make his food taste even better, to him.

"So you said your kids are eating at the farmhouse. You don't have parents, so...who?"

Her brows raised, and she finished chewing before she shook her head. "My oldest brother and his wife live in the farmhouse along with a couple of my unmarried siblings." It seemed like she didn't mind talking about it, and he had a deep-seated curiosity and wanted to find out everything he could about her.

"Interesting," he said. "I'm sorry about your parents."

She lifted her shoulder. "It was devastating, I'm not going to pretend it wasn't. And even to this day, it's been more than ten years, but I miss my mom. I miss being able to talk to her. There's so much I would like to ask her advice on and just things I would like to show her, and I'd love for her to be able to talk to my kids and help raise them, but..." She shrugged. "That just wasn't the way the Lord had my life planned."

"You mean you think it was God's plan for your parents to die?" He gave an angry huff of breath. "What a terrible view of God."

She looked surprised. "Everything that happens to me only comes through to touch me with God's permission. So, He's not the orchestrator of evil, but God allows things into your life that He knows will make you a better person. He promises that He'll work everything out for your good and His glory. I can see how my parents' death has been worked out for my good. Over and over and over again."

"Their death was God's plan?" He just couldn't get over that. That God would plan to have something terrible happen. It was like God would plan to have Regina Blue steal his songs and humiliate him in the court of public opinion. And he was helpless to fight that. He couldn't, wouldn't, not for one second, believe that a loving, good God would have allowed something so brutal into his life.

"How do I know it wasn't God's plan? Am I God?"

"If God is good, He couldn't allow something terrible like that to leave twelve children motherless?"

"So some of the good things that happened because of my parents' death—my siblings and I are so much closer than we would have been. We had to work together. We all knew that if we didn't work, we would lose the farm. We were inspired to work because we wanted to continue our lifestyle, not because our parents just told us to. I think we all developed good work ethics because of it. I am a lot more mature. I had to grow up quickly, because I had siblings who were depending on me. I had to cook." She held up what was left of her hamburger. "If Mom had been alive, maybe I would have just let her cook for me, but I had to cook, and we made sure that our younger siblings all learned to cook, to clean, to keep house, and to work outside. Because we knew that life happened unexpectedly, and we never knew whether they would be put someplace where they would have to survive on their own."

"But was all that worth the loss of your parents?"

"I know I'll see my parents again. It's just that we're parted for a little while down here. But when I get to heaven, I will have all of this to talk about with my mom. We can talk about how she might have done things differently. Or she could say that maybe she wouldn't have done anything different and things in my life have worked out for good. I don't know. I just know I'm not going to question what or why God allows."

"I still don't think all the good that you're talking about was worth your parents' death."

"I'm not questioning God. I'm just going to trust Him. If He allowed it into my life, it is for my good and His glory. And we can disagree on that if you want to, but nothing you say will convince me otherwise, because the Bible says that's true. And as much as I respect you," she nodded her head at him, and it was the first hint of any kind that she had given that he might be a famous figure, "and as much as I like you, I will always believe that God will work everything for my good. Even the things that look horrific and bad." She paused for a moment. "Even my divorce."

She looked back down at her burger and then took a bite, with her eyes downcast. He got the feeling that she wasn't intending to say that last bit and kind of wished she could take it back.

He didn't blame her. It was obvious that the divorce had hurt her a lot. He supposed it was kind of funny that she was here by herself with two little kids running around and no husband in sight. He hadn't thought to ask her whether or not she had a husband. That should have been his concern right away. He shouldn't be eating here alone with her if she were married.

"I suppose there are good things to come out of your divorce too?" he asked, mostly because he was curious about what had gone on about her divorce. Not necessarily because he had been convinced that God was good even if He allowed bad things to happen.

"Yes, there are." She gave an understanding smile as she finished the last of her burger. She brushed her hands over her plate before she continued. "For a long time, I didn't think that anything good could come out of so much pain and suffering. But yes. Yes, I can see the good things that happened."

He managed to eat two burgers in the amount of time it took her to finish one, but he was annoyed because a voice in the back of his head told him that if she could take such a positive view of God and her divorce, he should reconsider his stance on Regina Blue and the good Lord. So, while he knew that he should stay and help with the dishes, he pushed back and stood up from the stool.

"I think I better get home."

Chapter Nine

"How did it go?" Ada asked as she met Priscilla at the door when she came to pick up her children.

"I thought it went pretty well, but he left rather abruptly. We started talking about religion, and that seemed to upset him."

Priscilla couldn't figure out what else might have caused the sudden change in Cooper. She thought they had been getting along fairly well. It wasn't as easy a camaraderie as it might have been had she been eating with her sisters or a close friend, but she felt like they were enjoying each other's company. Then, they started talking about whether or not God was good and whether good things could come out of bad situations, and he seemed to close down and run out.

Maybe she had been too emphatic about what she believed. She knew she was right because the Bible said so. But...

"You know how sometimes my siblings say that I have to be right? Or I pound in my point?"

Ada laughed. "Yes. I know exactly what you're talking about."

Ada's humor didn't really help her much. Maybe she did have a tendency to insist that her way was the correct way.

"I feel like I only do that if I have the Bible behind me, you know? If it's just my opinion, I could be wrong. But the Bible isn't wrong." She emphasized that last sentence, each word.

"It's true the Bible isn't wrong, but some people aren't as firmly grounded in that as you are. And sometimes when you say it like that, leaving people no room for escape, they feel boxed in. I'm just guessing, since you and I are in total agreement on that."

"I know." After all, Priscilla had helped to teach Ada. Even though Ada was the closest girl in age to her, she was still five years younger.

Although, Ada had always seemed mature for her age and had always seemed to have a grasp of the Bible that had astounded Priscilla at times. That was one of the things that she wouldn't mind talking to her mother about. As they grew up, she wondered if it was normal the things that Ada seemed to know and naturally do. None of her other siblings had taken to a life of righteousness the way Ada had.

"I figured that you might be later, and I went ahead and told your kids to take showers. They were willing to do that because they thought they might get some extra reading time with their mom tonight." Ada gave her a smile that said she better follow through on that or they might not go home clean the next time.

"I understand," she said, calling her children and telling them it was time to go.

"Did you guys set up another time? Or is he going to eat hamburgers all winter?" Ada asked as she handed Justin's jacket to him and then grabbed Zaylee's jacket and helped her get it on.

"We didn't talk about it. I am not sure honestly." She wasn't sure why he left, why he was upset, or whether he was going to be back. She just wasn't sure. But for her part, she could try to be a little less emphatic when stating her opinion, even if it was based on what the Bible said, and not shove it down people's throats. She got the impression that maybe Cooper wasn't even a believer. Sometimes, being around her great big family where everyone was a Christian, although all of them were sinners too, left her with the impression that most of the world believed the way she did. When she knew, for a fact, that the exact opposite was true. The Bible said that too, that wide was the way that led to destruction and many walked that way, but narrow was the way that led to life, and few there be that found it.

Still, she told herself that she was going to try to be careful from then on to make sure that she did not box people in and make them feel like her way was the only way, even if she knew she was speaking from the Bible. Although, when she was talking to Christians, she felt she could stand on the Bible. Couldn't she?

She thought about that some as she shopped for groceries on Friday and took them to Cooper's cabin. She noticed that he ordered three one-pound packages of hamburger.

Along with lettuce and onion and tomatoes and rolls. She also noted the addition of mayonnaise in his order.

She really shouldn't be snooping in his food, but technically, she wasn't. She was just shopping for it. And if she noticed that he ordered some different things, it was normal. But her thinking about it probably could be curtailed. After all, he wasn't any of her business.

Her older brothers had told her that Cooper had been out and about on the ranch some that week with the bandage on his finger and an explanation that he hadn't been able to play his guitar so he needed to get out.

She had not seen him.

She did note the bandage still on his finger as he walked out on the porch when she pulled up beside his truck. He'd been out on the ranch when she'd cleaned on Monday and she hadn't seen him.

"I can get those," he called out as she waved and then opened the back door to start getting groceries out.

"I don't mind carrying some things in. There'll be plenty left for you."

He stepped off the porch and came in behind her.

"How's your finger?" she asked as she stood back with two bags in each hand, which was not nearly as many as she would have carried had he not been there.

"It's sore. You were right. It hurt a lot worse the next day, and the next day, and the next day."

"And today?"

"Yeah. I wish I'd had you get pain meds for me."

"Wow. That bad?"

"It wasn't really that bad, but I think I would have felt better if I would have had them beside me. You know, knowing I can take them if I need them, so no matter how bad it gets, I can handle it."

She walked away, carrying the bags up the steps and into the house. She had deliberately grabbed the refrigerated stuff so she could stick it in the refrigerator and not stay too long.

But today, he seemed to want to talk, since he brought the groceries and set them on the counter and said, "That's it." Then, instead of backing off like he usually did, he started getting things out and working beside her to put them away. She worked on the refrigerated things; he put things in the cupboard.

"I'm excited to be able to try to cook my own hamburgers. That's what I'm having for supper tonight."

"That's awesome," she said.

"You never told me how much I owed you for your help."

"I believe I told you that I was not going to allow a man who lived beside me to starve to death, and it was my pleasure to help."

"Well, I can't ask you to teach me another meal until I figure out how much I owe you for the last one. But hamburgers are going to get old pretty fast, I think."

"You know what days I'm free. And I'm happy to help you. Just name your time." She spoke simply. And it was true. She'd had a good time with him. And she was willing to give him a hand anytime she was able. Part of her wanted to ask why he'd run away, but he was acting like everything was okay, so maybe it was something he'd needed to work out himself. She had been planning on apologizing for being too pushy.

"Well, maybe you can think about what I can pay you, and I'll plan on coming on Saturday afternoon again."

"All right. Do you have anything specific in mind you'd like to learn to make?"

"Eggs are pretty easy, and they're healthy too. Maybe omelets?"

"All right. Omelets it is. On Saturday. Do you mind if my kids are there?"

"I don't mind at all," he said.

"They might prefer to be at the farmhouse, but I'll send them away if they're going to be a bother."

"I'm not used to being around kids. I realize that I haven't spent much time with them. And the kids I was around when I was younger were annoying. But maybe that was me. You know at times you get confused about how you view the world, and you assume that the way you view the world is the way everyone views the world?"

"Yes. I thought about that after you left so abruptly last week. I thought that maybe I had been too emphatic about what I believed. And while I feel like I have the facts to stand on, I wasn't very considerate about allowing you room to have your opinion."

"No. I just didn't want to hear your opinion. Because I know it's right, and I'm not ready to admit that some things that happened in my life were allowed to happen by God."

His voice was subdued, almost sad, and she thought that maybe what he was saying was whatever had happened that had caused him to need to leave the public eye for a little bit had been allowed by God. He wasn't ready to think that maybe God had meant that for good.

"Well, you don't have to give me more credit than I deserve. I know that I can be rather insistent that I'm right. My family laughs about it sometimes."

"It must be hard having so many people in your life who can laugh at you." He closed the cupboard door and turned around, folding his arms over his chest and giving her a steady look.

She put the last of the butter in the refrigerator and closed it as well.

She felt kind of odd to stand there in the kitchen, but he was looking at her like he wanted to say something else, and she felt it would be almost rude for her to walk away.

"Do you mind if I tell you something?"

"Sure."

"Do you have a few minutes?"

"I do."

"Your kids are taken care of?"

"That's always my first priority. Neither one of them really like to go grocery shopping, and I don't mind making them go grocery shopping for us and making them carry the stuff out and help me carry it in and put it away, but when I do it for you, I kind of feel like I should let my kids off the hook."

She often wondered if maybe she was being just a little bit too lenient with her children. She remembered helping her mom shop, and she also remembered helping her mom help other people. There was a lady who had been in a wheelchair that her mom went and did cleaning for in places where the lady couldn't reach. Windows and doorjambs and that type of thing. And she'd always taken one of her kids along with her, sometimes several. And they were put to work, either talking to the lady and keeping her company, or doing work that was more on their level, like lower cupboards or bathrooms.

"I'm not sure that we can make our kids work too much. I guess maybe concentration camp level of work might be a little bit overdoing it, but I don't think that overwork is something that plagues most American children today."

"I have to agree with that," she said, realizing that they did have a little bit of common ground.

"First of all, I wanted to apologize for leaving so abruptly last week," he said.

"It's not a problem. I just figured you probably weren't a believer and I was pushing you."

"No. I am a believer, and like I said, you were saying exactly what I knew to be true, I just wasn't ready to accept it."

"I think I went for years before I was ready to accept some truths."

"Then you understand."

She inclined her head but didn't say anything. He still hadn't gotten to what he really wanted to say.

She shoved her hands in her pockets and shifted on one foot.

"Would you like to sit down?" he asked, gesturing toward the kitchen or living room. She wasn't sure which, since they were both in that direction.

"If it's going to take a long time, I can."

"I would rather you be comfortable, because... I'm a little uncomfortable."

"Okay," she said. For the first time, a feeling of trepidation seemed to run through her. What was he getting at that made him feel uncomfortable?

She walked to the living room and perched on the edge of the couch.

He paced for a bit, and then he sat down on the other edge, still not looking completely at ease.

"So, you probably heard some of the things that happened to me during my last tour with Regina Blue."

"I have," she admitted, although she wanted to defend herself and say that she hadn't read the details on anything. Because she didn't want to jump to conclusions.

"All right then, part of the problem was that when she and I talked, we discussed a lot of songwriting things, and I even wrote some songs while she was around. She was not a muse exactly, but I would be sitting there with my guitar strumming and working on lyrics and that type of thing, and she would come and hang around and say 'that sounded good' and that type of thing. But I was always the one who came up with the words. Every word that I claimed is mine was mine."

"I believe you," she said, because it seemed important to him.

"After everything went down, I wasn't able to write at all. I had nothing. And I've made my living writing my own songs. I've never sung someone else's. I just...don't know how. The song is in me, it comes for me, and that's how I'm able to give life to it."

"Okay. I suppose that's a musician thing, because I don't really understand that, but I accept it."

He nodded, as though her words were good enough. "Like I said, I had nothing. Not a word, not a melody, not anything, until you came to my door. And then, it's like the dam in my head broke loose. And I had words, I had melodies, I had crazy amounts of everything. And then, when you walked out, it all stopped. So whatever I didn't capture while you were there or shortly after you left, I didn't get."

"Okay." That seemed a little weird, but who was she to question someone's creativity? She really didn't have a whole lot of her own, nothing tied to things like singing and music. She could draw okay, and she could make things look beautiful in the home. Make food look beautiful on a plate. And she enjoyed doing those kinds of things. But it wasn't something that she had to wait around for the muse to strike. Just something she did because she liked pretty things.

"So, when you're here cleaning, when you're here delivering

groceries, right now actually, I have music in my head. And it's happened every single time I've seen you."

"Interesting," she said. She wasn't quite sure how she felt about that.

"So, I was hoping that you would be willing to spend some time with me, just...like we're doing, only I might be writing some lyrics down and creating music while we are together."

"Like while I'm teaching you to cook?" she asked, since that was the next time they were going to be together.

"Yeah. Like then."

"That's fine with me."

His head went up and down, and then he looked out the window for a minute before he said, "It's scary for me to talk about this, because the last person who I wrote music around, it happened to be a woman, stole everything from me and then accused me of trying to steal her music, when it was mine to begin with."

"You don't have to worry about that with me. I'm not stealing anything, and I'm not trying to make music in any way. In fact, I'm not even sure I can sing well enough where someone would actually want to hear me. I've sung in the choir in church, but that's more because they needed people than because I actually was a good singer."

He nodded, barely cracking a smile over her little joke. "That's kind of what I figured. Then maybe I would be safe. But I feel like I owe you. You're teaching me to cook, and now you're going to willingly be my muse. I need to do something in return."

"I don't need anything. I'm just totally happy the way I am. Seriously, I know that sounds crazy, but my family pays me for what I'm doing for you, so if anything, you could offer to pay my brother more. I guess. But I've been through..." She paused for a moment, not wanting to go through all the trials and troubles that she'd been through. "I guess just a lot of pain and suffering, and to be here on the ranch, with my kids, with a house that I don't have to worry about whether or not I'm going to have the money to pay for, and enough to buy food, and I get to homeschool my kids, I get honest work to do, I have great people to work with, I have babysitters for my kids anytime I need them... I'm happy. I don't need anything."

She realized that was all true. And she realized what she had been trying to say about God being good. It truly was that, maybe if she had stayed married, she would still be striving for more and more and more the way she used to, but she didn't care anymore. It didn't matter. She was completely content with what God had given her, and she knew how valuable what she had right now was. To have her children, to have her family, to have a good job, and a great home, and she just couldn't be happier. She didn't want for anything. And it was all because of God and the trials that she had been through. Maybe she wouldn't appreciate things like she did now if she hadn't gone through what she had.

"Well, I guess I don't want to hear that, because I feel like if I take from you and I don't give back, then we're not square. Does that make sense?"

"That sounds like your childhood coming out in you."

"You're right. It's my grandmother. I can hear her saying that you want to make sure that you pay people back."

"That's fine, and I don't disagree with her in most instances, but in this instance, don't worry about it. We're good."

"If you think of anything that I can do for you, would you let me know?"

"Of course." She smiled. And the thought of her vlog went through her head. It would be really fun, as Ada had suggested, to have him on it, to show her teaching him how to cook, and to show that on her vlog, but she knew he didn't want to be in the public eye, and she wouldn't ask him for that.

Although, there was a part of her that wanted to, just to see if he truly meant what he said—that he would pay her back.

But a bigger part of her didn't want him to do something that he didn't want to do, and she was one-hundred-percent sure he did not want to do that.

"All right. That was all I had to ask. So, I'll bring my guitar when we meet, and I'll pay attention to you teaching me, but I might also be writing."

"Do you have a song right now?" she asked, curious.

"I do. It's a new one. Sometimes when you come, it's a continuation of the songs that I've started, but this is one I haven't heard before. I wondered if I walked into your house, if the song that started when we were there last Saturday would still be there, or if a new one would start. It's not super helpful if I only get snippets of a different song every time."

"Too bad you can't figure out a way to harness and control that."

"I think that's why it's called creativity. There isn't a whole lot of control. At least I don't have much. I know some people who can just schedule a time to sit down and knock out a song, like it's not a big deal. But my writing doesn't work that way."

"Interesting point that everyone is different."

She stood to her feet, and he followed her out.

"Don't forget. If there's anything I can do for you..."

He let his words trail off, but she shook her head. "Maybe someday there will be something, but I'm good for now."

She couldn't believe it; she was his muse? And he was offering to help her if she needed it? What a switch in their relationship. She certainly was not expecting that when she was grocery shopping for him that morning. In fact, she had been more concerned that he was upset with her and wasn't going to let her in.

With a wave and a promise to see him the next afternoon, she let herself out, still shaking her head at the turns life took sometimes.

Chapter Ten

"Steer!" Tobias called, and Cooper hurried to the steer pen gate, unlatching it and swinging it just in time to let the animal run through.

Ezra had invited him to watch as they were working cattle Saturday morning, and somehow the invitation had morphed into him helping.

Not that he minded. It was work to do with a hurt finger. He had tried to play his guitar several times, and the bandage got in the way. If he tried to take it off, it started bleeding as soon as he pressed the strings, and the pain was terrible.

He could stand the pain, but his creativity got zapped completely, plus with the blood everywhere, he couldn't write songs.

And that was the whole point.

Still, he managed to get down the song that had come to his head while he'd been cooking with Priscilla.

And he had to admit there was a very selfish part of him that was excited about their new agreement.

But the part of him that had been raised by his grandmother said that he needed to find something he could do in order to pay her back.

Helping on her ranch seemed like a small thing. And he wasn't helping Priscilla directly, the way she was him.

"Heifer!" someone yelled, and he had about a second and a half to run to the other gate and open it before a fast-moving bovine came around the corner and into view.

They had given him a job where he was almost certain not to get hurt as long as he kept himself out of the reach of flying hooves. More than one young animal had gone into the pen, kicking up their heels behind them.

One of them had actually hit the gate with their feet, but thankfully Cooper's fingers had been out of the way.

Of course, his job was nothing compared to what the other guys were doing. Some of them wrestled the animals into the chute, and it looked like one was giving shots, and another was dehorning the animals that needed it. Apparently they had crossbred with an unpolled breed, polled meaning naturally hornless, which was something that Cooper had learned that morning, and some of the second-generation animals now had horns.

None of those jobs were jobs he'd be able to do, at least not on his first day, but the gatekeeper job was exactly his speed.

As long as he could remember which pen had the steers in it and which pen had the heifers. Once he'd opened the wrong gate, and there was currently a steer in with the heifers.

The guys had told him not to worry about it, that they would sort it out at the end, since he had immediately gone to the middle of the herd and stood there.

He wasn't sure how they were going to sort it out, other than perhaps by using the dog that had been running around, especially at the beginning as they were getting the animals herded in.

It seemed to be rather well-trained and capable of cutting out an animal.

There were a couple of guys on horses too, and Cooper had been introduced to them. Most of them were brothers, but a couple were brothers-in-law.

A couple of the ladies were helping as well, but he hadn't seen Priscilla.

His stomach was rumbling, and he hoped lunch was going to be provided or that he was going to have time to go home and try out his new hamburger-making skills.

Priscilla had been right. Cooking wasn't that hard.

"Steer!" He was already standing at that gate, so it was easy to open it, and the animal ran in before Cooper closed the gate behind him.

The Clybourns seemed to be having a really good time, laughing and joking and including him in their conversations as much as they could.

It definitely did not feel exclusive, and he didn't feel looked down on just because he didn't have a whole lot of cattle ranching skills.

He remembered what Priscilla had said about her family losing her parents at a young age. And her siblings learning to work together as a result of it. Maybe that's what was going on now. Her family worked together because they hadn't had a choice if they had wanted to survive.

"Heifer!" The call came, and the animal came rushing around the corner.

He grabbed the gate, opened it, and closed it after her.

"You've been doing a great job. Three more, and the ladies have lunch ready. We're going to quit for a bit and refuel."

He was pretty sure it was Lucas, one of the brothers, who spoke, and he nodded.

"I'm ready," he said with a grin.

Lucas grinned back. "You and me both," he said, and he was laughing as he disappeared back around toward the chute.

The last three went quickly, and he carefully closed the pen behind the last steer, walking over to where the men stood, getting food on the table. Sandwiches were wrapped in aluminum foil, and they were hot since steam rolled off of them as the guys opened them.

A hot meal. He wasn't expecting that. If they were going to bring it out, he would assume it was going to be cold sandwiches.

Thankfully, it wasn't that cold outside, although in his opinion, it was sweater weather. Several of the guys worked in T-shirts, and maybe if he had a more strenuous job, he would have decided to switch as well. Most of them had flannels on, although others wore sweatshirts just as he did.

"I appreciate your help. We'll find you better footwear if you're going to make a habit of helping us." Tobias, another brother he'd just met that morning, eyed Cooper's cowboy boots.

"I didn't realize you guys were going to put me to work. Priscilla invited me to walk around the ranch, saying that I would be welcome to nose around. She didn't add I'd get put to work." He figured he could rib them just as much as they were ribbing him.

"On workdays, we have a tendency to grab whoever's wandering around and give them a purpose in life. It's...a calling," Lucas said, making everyone else laugh. Lucas seemed to be a bit of a jokester.

"That's what happened to me. I was just minding my own business, and they basically kidnapped me and put me in their chain gang."

He was pretty sure that was Stonewall, who had married into the family.

"That's his side of the story. The actual truth is that he started hanging around, and we couldn't get rid of him, so we figured we might as well start making him earn his keep, because he ate enough for three people."

That was Asher, another brother.

At first, all the brothers had looked the same, but he was starting to be able to differentiate between them. Some of them were serious, some seemed like they were goof-offs, but they all had an easygoing acceptance that made working with them fun. Even though not everything had gone according to plan, no one had lost their temper, and there hadn't been any yelling or meanness. It was the kind of place he didn't mind working.

Cooper looked around for a drink after picking up a sandwich. He saw Priscilla over at the side, talking to one of her brothers. It looked like Ezra.

He wanted to go over and say something to her. After all, she was the one person here that he knew rather well. That he'd seen more than once or twice. She was in his cabin twice a week, and now, he was visiting her as well.

Interestingly, he didn't even need to walk over for a piece of a song to flit through his mind.

This one was less of a love story and more a hardworking, middle

American song. Perfect for his genre of music, and perfect for his audience.

He wished he would have thought to stick a notebook and a pen in his pocket.

He hummed the melody, no longer surprised that the words came with their own music. It was something that just happened when Priscilla was around.

She finished chatting with Ezra, and Cooper grabbed a drink as he walked over, catching her as she started heading back toward the house.

"Hey there," he said, and she stopped, turning with a smile.

"Cooper. I see my brothers put you to work."

"Oh, you saw that?" She must have been there before they took a break in order for her to see that he was actually working. For some reason, he was happy that he hadn't been standing around with his hands in his pockets. He wasn't quite sure why. There was no shame in that, considering that this wasn't his ranch and this wasn't his livelihood. He hadn't done anything like this ever before in his life, despite growing up on a farm. Their cattle operation had not been big enough for this type of work.

"Yeah. I was up for a bit to bring the second herd up and to cut the young calves out."

"I haven't seen any young calves."

"Then I did my job," she said with a laugh.

"Seriously. Are there babies somewhere?"

"We have some cows that calved in August, and then we have some of our herd that are calving now. It's just because of the things we're doing. Normally we don't do it that way. But anyway, the August babies are a little bit older, but we do have some young newborns. And you shouldn't have seen any of those."

"Well. I guess you're right. You did your job, because I haven't. So far anyway." He grinned. "Now that I know you were the one responsible, I'll keep my eye out for them."

"If you see any, be sure to tell the boss. Maybe I'll get fired." She laughed, like the idea was funny. What must it be like to work for your family and know that your job security was totally in the bag? But that didn't mean that she didn't do a good job. She cleaned his house, and it was spotless. She made his bed, and it looked like she'd done it for inspection at boot camp, and his groceries were always perfect. She didn't forget a thing, and even when she'd been teaching him how to cook, she'd done it well. She was friendly and kind without being inappropriate in any way.

More lyrics twisted around in his mind, and he thought that maybe the original song was going to turn out to be a love song anyway.

That seemed to be what he wrote when he was around Priscilla.

"Are you thinking of lyrics now?" she asked, tilting her head after he hadn't said anything for a while, just standing there like a fool, sandwich in one hand, water in the other, and staring at her.

"Is it that obvious?" he asked, even though he knew it was.

Priscilla lifted her brows and moved her eyes to the side, like she was trying to think of something to say that wasn't total agreement. Finally, she shrugged. "Yeah. It's that obvious. You get this look in your eyes, and you just space out." She laughed, the sound floating on the air and causing even more lyrics to march into his brain and across his vision. "It's a little bit weird to know that when you look at me, you don't really see me; you're thinking about songs."

He realized then that he was going to be writing in front of her, and she would know the songs in his head were love songs.

He wasn't sure that he wanted her to know that. And he didn't quite understand why other than she might get the wrong impression. After all, he wasn't interested in her in that way.

Right?

He didn't want to examine it too much. Because sometimes the way the songs came out, it was like he was thinking. But was that really where his mind was going when he was around Priscilla?

No. He couldn't allow it to go in that direction at all. He had already been burned by one woman who had stolen everything from him. He wasn't going to allow that to happen again. No matter how sweet and nice this one seemed.

"I'm sorry it's weirding you out," he finally said, shoving away the thoughts that had been plowing through his mind. "I just wish I had a pen and a piece of paper. I would be writing these things down."

"I'll grab some out of the bunkhouse when I'm back there and bring them to you."

"All right. I'll probably have more." If she was around. "At least that's pretty much the way it's been going lately."

"Okay," she said, still looking like she didn't quite believe that she was the reason that he was writing songs.

He really wanted to get the subject off him though. He was interested in knowing more about her. Maybe after seeing her working on the ranch, or hearing about her parents, or just knowing that she was helping him get back into the groove of what he needed to do for a living had made him curious about her.

"Have you thought about what I can do to pay you back for what you're doing for me?" he asked, shoving his water in his back pocket and opening up the sandwich. He wasn't sure how long the guys were going to stop for lunch, but he didn't want to miss his opportunity to eat.

"I told you. You don't need to pay me back. The idea is a little bit annoying. Like, I can do something nice for you and you don't have to act like you can't just accept it."

"I don't usually let strangers just walk into my life and start giving me stuff." She didn't understand how valuable what she was doing was.

"Am I really still a stranger? We've been talking to each other now for almost three weeks. Surely I've moved to at least casual acquaintance. If not friend?"

He looked at her. He would like to have a friend like her. Someone who seemed too pure to do anything underhanded.

But Regina Blue hadn't exactly screamed liar and cheater either.

"I suppose we could be casual friends," he said, not wanting to insult her by telling her that he was very choosy about the people that he allowed into his friendship circle.

This whole family just seemed to be something from decades ago, rather than a modern family. Typically there was some kind of dysfunction in every family. Tempers, fights, drama. But so far at least, he hadn't experienced any of that.

"Do you guys really just get along all the time?" he asked, taking a bite of his sandwich and appreciating the warmth. It was delicious too. Of course, with Priscilla involved, he wouldn't have expected anything else. Somehow he got the idea in his head that she did everything well.

"We have our times. We often have times where we rub each other the wrong way. But we figured out from a really young age that if this was going to work, nobody could get their way all the time. Now, sometimes there's some grumbling that some people get their way a lot more than other people, and I suppose that's true to some extent."

"Ezra?"

"He's more like the leader. He listens to everyone, and then he makes the best decision, and so far, he hasn't steered us wrong. Maybe someday, the other brothers will get tired of him always being the one in charge and will challenge him..." Her words faded off and were thoughtful, almost as though she hoped the day never came or that she didn't think about it often. "But I guess what happens happens. And I'm not going to worry about it."

That seemed to be her theme song. That she wasn't going to worry about things. And he felt like that was probably a good one.

"What song are you thinking about?" she asked, bringing the conversation back to him.

"I was trying not to think about songs. I don't have any way of writing anything down, and it just gets annoying when they're stuck in my head, and I know I'm going to lose them, and I keep thinking about what a great song it is."

"I'll head out to the bunkhouse, and I'll be back shortly with a notebook and a pen. Hopefully one that will fit in your pocket."

"I should have worn a flannel. I would have a pocket right here for my notebook." He patted his chest and then stuck the rest of the sandwich in his mouth.

"These are really good, by the way," he said, realizing he talked with his mouth full but wanting to let her know before she disappeared.

"Thanks. Ada and I were the two that made them. Usually Alaska is in charge of the food, but today she got to help, because Sondra and Ryland are watching kids."

He assumed that those were sisters or sisters-in-law. "Alaska?"

"She's Ezra's wife."

She must have been the one running around with the tattoos on her arms. She had her sweatshirt off for a while, and he'd wondered how she had become a part of this family that seemed so clean-cut.

But he wasn't fooled for a second to think that there weren't problems in the family. Priscilla had hinted at it and had flat-out said that sometimes they didn't get along. He was sure that there were other things as well. Every family had problems. No family was perfect. But when people set aside their differences and tried to get along, it was pretty amazing what they could accomplish.

"I'll be back," Priscilla promised, and then she gave him a jaunty wave and hurried toward a building in the distance.

That must be the bunkhouse.

Maybe he could ask her for a tour. Now that he was moving around more, it would probably be a good idea for him to know where things were and what their purpose was. He also wouldn't mind getting to know everyone better.

Chapter Eleven

"How's your social media doing?" Ada asked as she and Priscilla stood at the fence, feet propped up, leaning against the top rail, watching the men work.

Their job for the day was done. They still had a few dishes to clean up, but supper was in the crockpots, lunch was over, and they had a little bit of time to stand around and chat.

Priscilla had delivered the notebook that Cooper had requested, along with a pen. And she even borrowed a flannel that had been lying in the bunkhouse. She thought it was Tobias's, but she wasn't sure. Whoever's it was, her brothers wouldn't care if she gave it to Cooper to wear.

He had thanked her, but he hadn't put it on.

She figured if he really wanted a pocket for his notebook, he'd have one. Otherwise, he could just set it aside and bring it back.

She picked at a splinter on the split rail fence. "It's doing okay. I'm up to twelve hundred subscribers."

"Wow. You got two hundred subscribers in the last three weeks?" Ada seemed very impressed with it.

"Yeah. I guess that's good, but it just feels so slow to me. You know?"

"Yeah. I get it. I guess for normal people, that's a pretty big jump, but you're trying to make money from it..."

"Yeah. It's not even enough to buy a cup of coffee every day. I thought it would be...not easier, just fall into place more?"

"If you're doing what you think God wants you to do, you think it's going to work out perfectly the first time, right?" Ada said as the guys opened the chute and yelled at Cooper to open the heifer pen.

From where they stood, they could see both the head chute, and their brothers working around it, and also Cooper around the corner, where he opened the pens up.

Cooper had been scribbling furiously a while back, but he had the notebook shoved back in his pocket, and as Priscilla watched, he took his sweatshirt off, shoving his arms in the flannel and buttoning it up.

She smiled. He was just waiting for a good time to change.

"Isn't that the way it's supposed to go? If God is in it, it's not necessarily easy. But if He's not, then you get roadblock after roadblock."

"Is that the way things are in the Bible? Is that what we think about the early Christians? Weren't they doing the right thing, and yet they were fed to the lions, boiled in oil, and persecuted to the point where they scattered all across the continent?"

"That's kind of a special case, isn't it?"

"Was everything easy for David? After he was anointed king, I mean, even that... His dad didn't even acknowledge that he was one of his sons when Samuel came to anoint him. Talk about a roadblock. You kinda have to be present in order to get anointed king."

Priscilla laughed. She supposed that was true, and then as she thought about the rest of David's life, how he had gone just to check on his brothers and taken food and ended up killing Goliath. That was easy enough, except the armor that he had been given had been too much, and he shrugged it off, plus his brothers had made fun of him and told him to go back to the sheep. It wasn't like everything just worked out perfectly.

"How long was it that he hid from Saul? It was years, wasn't it?" Ada asked, like she really couldn't remember.

"I guess you're right. He was in the palace some, and then Saul tried to kill him." She sighed. "Nobody's trying to kill me."

"Well, that's a relief," Ada said with a little bit of sarcasm in her voice. "Maybe, if someone does, you can let me know, okay? I'm your sister, and sisters need to know these things."

Priscilla laughed. Sometimes it felt like she and Ada were so much the same age. When they were younger, the five-year age gap between them seemed like a lifetime, but now, sometimes Ada almost felt older. She had passed on several men who had been interested in her, because they hadn't had the values or standards that she wanted in a husband. They were good men, just not what she was looking for.

Priscilla admired that. She really didn't know what she was looking for back when she was looking. Not that she was looking now. She just knew she wanted to get married and have a family, and she knew that her husband had to be a Christian. That was the only prerequisite the Bible gave for marriage specifically.

Still, she didn't think she necessarily had made an obvious blunder with her ex. He just turned out to not be what everyone thought he was. Maybe he wasn't even what he thought he was.

"If I find out that anyone's trying to kill me, I'll let you know," she conceded, trying to sound reluctant. Which made Ada laugh.

"I guess my point is, no. Just because it's God's will doesn't mean everything is just going to fall in place without effort. Everything in life takes effort. It all takes work. Even Jesus's ministry didn't fall in place without effort. He was kicked out of towns, people constantly tried to trick him, the religious leaders of the day hated him, and he lost followers all the time. It certainly wasn't a walk in the park. And that's not even counting the fact that when he was young, King Herod wanted to kill him so bad he gave an order to kill all of the young boys in that area of the country. His parents had to escape to Egypt for a time."

"All right. You're right. I guess... I guess I just think if I'm doing God's will, He's going to make it happen. But you're right. He hasn't done that for anyone throughout history. You always hear about Christians struggling and being persecuted and that type of thing. Things don't take off without a lot of time and work." She tried not to be discouraged. She hadn't exactly thought that God was just going to wave His magic wand and bless her because she was doing something good for Him. But she hadn't expected it to be quite so difficult.

Or slow.

"How are things going with Cooper? You haven't had any more cooking lessons since he sliced his finger bad enough to need stitches last time?"

"He's a stubborn man."

"Are those two words redundant?" They had enough brothers that they ought to know.

"All right. He's just a typical man, and he wouldn't go get stitches. But the cut was bad enough that he needed them."

"That sounds more like it."

"Yeah. We've agreed that he wants to be able to write songs while we're working together." It seemed a little weird to say that she was his muse or that she inspired his songwriting ability, so she left that part out. It seemed odd to her, and she wasn't sure she could explain it, and she definitely wasn't sure she believed it.

Although, she couldn't figure out why he'd be lying about it.

"And you don't think that's a little bit weird?" Ada finally asked. She should have known that Ada would think the same thing she was.

"I guess... I don't know how people write songs. I'm not a songwriter. And isn't it weird that I record myself going out to feed the calves every morning and I record exercises?"

"Sorry. But that's a little bit more normal."

"To us. Not everybody feeds calves every day. And not everybody writes songs while they're working. It's just... I don't know. Each to his own, I guess."

"I wasn't giving you a hard time. I just...didn't really understand it, I suppose."

They stood there watching the guys for a while. They had gotten to the point where they were working together smoothly, with everyone doing their job and things going well.

"It was always so much fun when things clicked like that," Ada said thoughtfully.

"I agree. I always loved working with cattle, except when you can't get cows in, or something got stuck, or—"

"It was freezing cold or stifling hot, or the flies were terrible."

They both laughed. There were all kinds of things that could throw a wrench in the works.

"Today is one of those golden days where everything goes well."

"So we do have days like that. But not every day is like that," Ada said, looking at Priscilla, as though she wanted to make sure that Priscilla understood.

"I agree. You are right." She grinned, and Ada bumped her shoulder with hers.

"Did I detect sarcasm in that answer?" she asked, laughing.

"Perhaps?" she said, still grinning. Then her grin faded. "Do you think you'll ever get married?" She hadn't planned to ask that, but it had been a question that had been nagging her for a while. Ada had so much to offer someone. She was beautiful. Priscilla had always considered her the most beautiful sister. She had a natural grace about her that Priscilla had always envied as well. And she was funny and smart.

"I guess I can't say God's gonna have to make it easy for me when I just gave you a lecture about how God doesn't make things easy."

"Exactly," Priscilla said, nodding decisively.

"I just haven't felt like any of the men that have been around and have been interested have been the man God wanted for me. I don't know... Maybe I'm expecting too much. But I feel like when the right man comes along, I'm going to know it. God's gonna somehow tell me. Is that too pie-in-the-sky thinking?"

"I don't know. I felt like God told me for sure that I was supposed to get married. Our parents agreed. Our brothers thought it was okay. It was like all the stars lined up. And look at me."

"It's hard to think that God lined that all up, so you could go through what you went through. Do you think that's possible?"

"I think it's possible because God works everything out for our good and His glory." She didn't used to believe that. In fact, when she was at the depths of her pain, not seeing her children, with no hope of ever being with her family and having her children too, she didn't believe that at all. "Sometimes it just takes a while, and it's hard to see. But I do believe that everything works out for good. Whether or not God orchestrated the divorce... I don't know." She looked at her shoulder.

"It's hard to imagine God, who hates divorce, deciding that it was okay for it to happen so that He can teach me a few lessons, but—" She stopped for a moment.

Ada picked up where she left off. "You're a lot different person than you used to be. You grew a lot, learned a lot, and it's like your divorce was the refining fire that caused you to grow closer to the Lord and become a more pure Christian."

"That's exactly what I was thinking. So did God plan it? I don't think so. Did God allow it? Most definitely. Did God work it out for my good? Absolutely."

She believed that with all of her heart. But she thought again about her conversation with Cooper and how he didn't. She supposed he was right. Did God really orchestrate sin? She didn't think He did. But He could bring good out of it every single time.

The Bible was full of stories of men who had other men sin against them, and God worked it out for good.

The underlying idea for her was that: God was in everything. It might not be His plan, but He was in it. And nothing touched her except with God's express knowledge and permission.

Chapter Twelve

Cooper walked into Priscilla's house, whistling the song he'd written earlier in the week when she'd come to clean his house. It was one of his favorite songs so far out of the ten or so he'd been able to write in the last six weeks.

He couldn't believe what six weeks could do to a person. He felt so much better. The pastor he'd been watching online had been talking about forgiveness—timely, as God usually was—and Cooper had to admit that it felt so much better to let the past go and not hold onto it.

When the pastor had said that God had commanded forgiveness as much for the person who was doing the forgiving as anything, it had struck home with him. He wanted Regina Blue to suffer from what she had done, but the only person he was making suffer was himself through his bitterness and lack of forgiveness.

Sometimes, once or twice at least, he'd even gotten a few song lyrics written when Priscilla wasn't around. He thought for sure that was a sign of how much healing he had done.

"Your kids aren't here today?" he asked, as he looked around and it was just Priscilla standing at the counter, finishing up a few dishes.

"We're making mashed potatoes. Alaska's making cookies. It was a no-brainer for my children."

"You know, you could have changed the menu at the last minute. I certainly wouldn't have complained about that."

Surely she didn't think he would mind making cookies? Even though he would never make them as a meal.

Would he?

As he got older, he tried to be more mindful of what he ate. It seemed like when he was young, the impurities and junk that he put into his body didn't seem to matter, but the older he got, the more he thought about it.

Still, a supper of cookies wouldn't hurt if he didn't make a habit of it. Although, if he were being perfectly honest, cooking was work, and he wasn't sure he would go through that much work just to make himself a meal of junk food.

"You know, if nothing else, the last six weeks working with you as you showed me how to cook, and then cooking for myself, has made me appreciate every meal that someone else makes for me. Because not only is there work involved in cooking the meal, but you have to clean up the dishes that you got dirty in making it, and then you have to clean up the dishes involved in eating it. And then you have to put the food away!" He couldn't believe all the work he'd never thought about before.

"Don't forget there's the work of planning the meal, shopping for the ingredients, getting them, bringing them home, and putting them away. It starts long before the day you actually eat the meal."

All the things that she named were things that she had been doing for him. Of course, he decided what he was going to eat, so he did the planning, to a degree, since the meals he planned were all meals that she had chosen to teach him, but all the rest of it, she had been doing.

"And thank you so much for the work that you've done so I can eat." He thought for a moment. "And all that we just talked about doesn't include all the work of growing the food. Wow. Humans exist basically to just feed themselves."

"If you think about it, all roads point to that. You've got people who have jobs and earn money doing other things, but you have to spend the money on purchasing the food, and I guess you skip the steps of growing it yourself, but isn't that the first thing that you have to do with your money?"

"Food, clothing, and housing." He had never thought about things in such basic blocks before. He always thought about becoming a big star, about his music, and how he could change the world with it. He had never been concerned about something as simple as thinking about where his food came from.

"And the cornerstone of food is mashed potatoes," Priscilla said, laughing as she did so.

"For the Irish anyway," he said.

"You look like you might have a little Irish in you somewhere," she said, pretending like she was eyeing him.

They had settled into an easy camaraderie, which he appreciated. Now that she knew that she helped him write songs, she'd been totally fine with him grabbing his notebook and jotting some things down. He typically didn't bring his guitar when they cooked, but he almost always had it out when she came to his house. Most of the time, he sat in a corner just focusing on his music, every once in a while looking up at her to allow the words to run through his brain.

"Do you have a song today?"

"I've been so busy singing the song I wrote this week, which is one of my favorites ever, I haven't even thought about a new song."

"Resting on your laurels, are you?" she said with a smirk.

He smiled with her, but she acted like he didn't have laurels to rest on. And that didn't bother him, it just surprised him a little. He was used to people gathering around him and telling him how wonderful he was, not acting like he could accomplish so much more.

"I suppose in the grander scheme of things, writing songs and singing them really isn't that important," he said, unable to believe that for the first time, he'd seen his job as extraneous. "After all, we have to eat, we need shelter and clothes. That doesn't have anything to do with any of those three things."

"Don't you think human beings have a need for love and comfort and safety?" she asked, her brows puckering down like it wasn't something she thought about a lot, and she was thinking as she spoke. "And isn't that where music comes in? I mean, there's really no other animal or species in the world that has music. It's one thing, along with our thumbs, that makes us different." She wiggled her thumb before she grabbed the bag of potatoes.

"I've never thought about that either. Which is so weird, considering that music is my life." It wasn't that Priscilla was amazingly smart, and it wasn't that she was even a deep thinker. She just had a perspective that was different from his, even though they agreed on most of the same underlying principles.

"But I'm holding you up." He nodded at the potatoes in her hands. "I take it we're not making the instant kind?"

"That's not my job, is it?" she said with a laugh. "We're doing the homemade, made from scratch all the way meals."

"We're doing everything? As in, mixing up the...whatever ingredients it takes to make pasta?"

She laughed again, and he enjoyed their easy conversation. He also admired the sparkle in her eyes and the way she was never in a bad mood. Sure, he'd come in on days when she looked tired, or when she'd been worrying about a problem she had, usually with her kids and school, but she'd never allowed that to cause her to be anything but kind. He wished all of the people he worked with were that considerate of others.

"I think we'll cheat on the pasta," she said finally.

He watched as she showed him how to pare potatoes and explained that her mother always told her that she was to try to take off the least amount of skin as possible.

She couldn't believe it when he told her that he never pared potatoes.

"What about apples? Have you pared apples before?"

He shook his head. "No. We didn't pare them when I was little. We just picked them off the ground, rubbed them on our shirts, and then ate them, careful not to get a worm."

"So, he had a childhood after all." She said it with a lighthearted teasing that he knew wasn't a hint for him to give more information. But he realized that in all the time they'd been together, he hadn't really talked about his childhood.

"I didn't know you were interested."

"I figure it must be black and dark and terrible for you to avoid talking about it like you do."

"Someone has a pretty active imagination. Because there's really nothing black or dark or terrible about my childhood at all, except we were poor, and all I wanted to do was sing and make music, and as you can imagine, the adults in my life didn't think that I should spend every waking second doing that."

"I see. So your childhood was spent with you striving and fighting to play a guitar and your parents striving and fighting to get you to do school." She tilted her head and stopped paring for just a moment. "I can relate to your parents."

He laughed, knowing that she'd been having a little bit of trouble with Zaylee wanting to finish schoolwork. She hadn't discussed it with him, and he wouldn't know why she would. He didn't have the answers for her. But she had mentioned in passing that she was working on trying to find things that would motivate her.

She had laughed at the time, because she had said that for years, her biggest problem was that her children weren't with her, and now that that big problem was solved, she found other things to make into problems.

He had loved the way she put it into perspective. She also said that whether her kids were in school or whether they were homeschooled wasn't the most important thing to her. Because more than anything else, she wanted her children to know Jesus and to grow up to love and serve him. She felt like they needed to be able to read, and they needed to be able to do math. Beyond that, it wasn't that she wouldn't strive for her children to learn, because she felt it was important, obviously, since she was taking the time to homeschool. But she didn't feel like it was worth losing relationships over, and it was more important for her to find ways for the information to stick than to make him sit and do every last problem.

It felt like an innovative approach to teaching, one that he hadn't encountered in his years.

"I actually didn't have parents. My dad was never in the picture, and my mom moved to Hollywood to try to be an actress. She left me with my gram, who raised me and my two older siblings."

"You have older siblings?" she said with surprise, not looking up from her potato.

He was doing a terrible job with his potato. It looked like he was trying to make a sculpture out of it rather than trying to skin it. But he supposed that one got better with practice. At least with Priscilla helping him, this wasn't going to take all night. She had about six potatoes pared to his one. It would have taken him an hour to do it on his own.

"I do. A sister and a brother, who are not in the music business." He didn't know why everything came back to that. Other than maybe there were songs running through his head, and he was constantly thinking about that when he was with Priscilla. Not so much now that he couldn't have a conversation, especially since he was pretty confident that was going to continue to happen. He figured as long as the Lord gave it to him, he would take advantage of it.

"And you all grew up together with your gram? What about your grandfather?"

"He died relatively young, black lung."

She nodded, looking sad but not saying anything.

"That was before I went to live with her. So, it wasn't that I wasn't sad about it, I just didn't know. But Grandma lived on a small farm, so all of this—cows and horses and pigs and sheep and goats and all that— we had some of it, although not on the scale that you guys do."

"I've always thought that the West seems bigger than the east. Maybe that's just a preconceived notion I have, since I grew up out here, but that's the way it feels to me."

"I suppose that's true in a way. You guys have bigger mountains. Bigger open spaces. And it takes more ground to raise the same amount of things because you have less rain. But your houses are smaller."

She nodded and smiled, laughing just a little. "I can't argue with that," she said. "So you didn't enjoy growing up on the farm?"

"I suppose like most little kids, I enjoyed running around and playing. There were so many places to play. Playgrounds don't even scratch the surface of what's on a farm. I feel bad for the poor kids who only have playgrounds."

Playgrounds were fun, but they weren't anything compared to a farm. "But you're right. I didn't enjoy the chores, didn't enjoy the daily grind. There was always work to do. Especially with my gram being a single mom, older, and raising three unexpected children. I never even considered how much sacrifice that was for her and how much that must have weighed on her mind, whether or not she would be able to afford to feed us." He shrugged a shoulder. "Talking about our earlier conversation where it takes so much work just to feed yourself. A single widowed woman trying to raise three small children alone. Wow."

"But your gram is living in luxury now, right?" Priscilla said easily, and Cooper flinched.

"She passed away just as I was starting to make it big. My dream was always to make it so that she didn't have to work if she didn't want to. But honestly, I'm not sure she would have allowed me to do that. She loved what she did. She never really had much, but she was one of the happiest people I know. You remind me a lot of her."

Priscilla's head came up with that, and her eyes widened.

"In what way?" she asked as she finished paring the last potato.

"You're always happy. You always have a positive look on things. You don't take things at face value, but you realize that there might be another idea or another way, not to mention the care you show your children. There was never a question that my gram loved us fiercely and would fight for us. Although, she expected us to behave and expected us to work. Which I appreciate, or I never would have. She made sure that we knew that it was because she wanted us to grow up to be respectable adults and not a drain on society."

His gram was big on that. She didn't believe in welfare. It was one thing to give someone a helping hand. It was another thing to enable them to live a lifestyle of laziness and unproductiveness.

"I wasn't always happy. I'm still not. But I suppose that's another one of those things that Gram tried to teach me. That I get to choose whether or not I'm content and happy with my life. Now of course, a mother isn't going to be content away from her children, but... If you know that you've done everything you can, and you're just waiting for the Lord to move, sometimes you just have to be content in that valley for a bit. And it's much easier if you choose to be happy."

"And music helps that," she said easily, tying into something else that they had been talking about.

"It does indeed."

"All right. What you do now is cut the potatoes and put them in a pot to boil them." She gave him a side-glance. "Do not cut yourself with that knife. It's sharp."

He laughed, knowing that she probably wouldn't soon let him live that down. His finger had healed a long time ago, but every time they worked with a knife, she reminded him not to cut himself.

She showed him how to cut the first potato and explained that the smaller the chunks of potato were, the faster they would cook, which made sense.

"Now, once we have them in the pot and boiling, I want to show you one way to mash them, but we're going to do it differently today."

"All right." He put the lid on the pot and came over to stand beside her while she got her phone out and clicked a few buttons.

"I put this on my blog the other day. I have a stand mixer, and I use that to mash the potatoes. But today we're going to use a hand mixer. I just wanted you to be aware. Sometimes I assume things that I know are common knowledge, but I wouldn't be doing my job if I didn't at least mention this."

"I guess I knew that. Probably. But I've done this type of thing so seldom that it's good to know that there's two options." He glanced down as she pushed play, and he realized that it was her talking. It was her social media account. There were several hundred likes on the video, as well as comments.

"That's your social media account?" he asked as the video ended, and she pulled her phone away. It was much bigger than it had been a few weeks ago when he'd checked it out.

"Yes."

She set the phone down on the table and walked to the refrigerator, saying, "We're going to put some butter in these potatoes, and I also put sour cream and sometimes garlic in them as well. It depends on what we're serving them with and what kind of gravy is going along with it. I wasn't going to try to do the meat and gravy today though."

"That's the best part." And then, because he wasn't done talking about it, he said, "Do you make money on that?"

"My cooking? Or my social media?" she asked, turning around with a stick of butter and a tub of sour cream in her hand.

"The social media account." Several hundred likes wasn't that many. Not if a person was trying to earn anything from it.

"I do. Not a whole lot. Right now, I'm using it to buy Christmas presents for the kids, and once I hit my budget for each of the kids, which isn't that high, I'm going to use it to buy gifts for my nieces and nephews, and then Whitney has an in with the school, and she knows several kids who aren't going to have a very big Christmas. So, I figured I would take my children shopping, and we would grab some things for them." She smiled. "Big dreams, since I don't even have half of my budget earned for my own children. But I thought I might talk to them about having less and giving more."

"I don't think you want to do that," he murmured, but he was thinking. He knew a way to get her blog a lot more exposure. He'd known she'd been working on it for a while. And the idea had been percolating in his mind. He just didn't want to. He didn't want to expose himself like that. Except he really was feeling better. And it would kind of be like him doing something for a good cause and paying her back at the same time.

"No. I feel like the kids might really get a lot of pleasure out of it. And we don't have a lot of room here. So it's not like we can get a ton of things. Where are we going to keep it all? Also, I've seen throughout my life that when God gives me something, and I give part of it away, giving it back to the Lord or giving to other people, God gives me more and more and more. I just sometimes have to stand in disbelief at how God has provided for me, especially when I've given what I didn't think I had to give. You know?"

He nodded, but he really didn't know. Sure, he gave to charities, but it was money that he didn't mind giving. And he didn't really need it for himself. He had more than enough to sustain his lifestyle for the rest of his life. He didn't need millions and gazillions more. Except, every time he started making more, somehow he started spending more. On himself.

Maybe that was why God had taken everything away from him for a while. To show him that while he had had good intentions when he started out of giving money to his gram, after she passed away, he hadn't looked around for anyone else that he could give a helping hand to.

That was on him.

She set the butter down on the cutting board and used the knife to cut it into small pieces. "Sometimes my children have surprised me with the way they've internalized the things that I've taught them. And sometimes they surprise me by the way they see things." She lifted her eyes, her hands not moving for a moment on the butter. "I figure if Whitney gives us the names of kids that they know, and they start to think about how those kids maybe don't have the family they do or how their homelife isn't as good as what my kids have, they might decide on their own that they want to try to do something for them."

"So you're not dreaming of making it rich with your social media?"

She laughed. "No. Who would want to see me do anything? The idea that anyone does even a little is kind of laughable to me. I'm so ordinary."

He disagreed. He thought she was extraordinary. The more time he spent around her, the more he truly believed that. She didn't know how one of a kind she was.

Did he realize how truly one of a kind she was? And if he did, why wasn't he doing something about it?

The old fears of not being able to trust and of having everything stolen from him by someone who smiled to his face and then drove the knife deep into his back came rushing back, but Priscilla wasn't that kind of person. It was so obvious after spending as much time with her as he had that there was no way she would ever do that to someone.

Still, he couldn't bring himself to offer his presence. He knew all she needed to do was take a video of him in her kitchen and post it online, and it was sure to be spread around, going viral beyond her wildest dreams most likely. Not that he had an inflated idea of what his name was capable of, but he'd experienced that himself, and it was true.

He felt guilty that he was withholding something from someone who'd given him so much. He thought of the ten songs he had written because of her and her willingness to help him however she could. Her cheerful attitude, her easy acceptance of life, and the way she was completely okay with the small amount of money that her videos were making online.

Why didn't he open his mouth and let her know he could help?

<h1 style="text-align:center">Chapter Thirteen</h1>

Cooper felt guilty about not offering to use his name to help Priscilla. He found himself thinking about saying something to Ezra the next time they were working together, going out along the fence line and checking it. They had found the spot where the cattle had pushed down on it and created a gaping hole.

"Pretty soon we'll be having calves get out here, if not cows."

"Seems like the grass is always greener on the other side of the fence," Cooper said, figuring that Ezra had figured that out a thousand times over, and he was just now realizing the truth of that statement.

"It's ninety percent of the reason for broken-down fences," Ezra said, laughing.

They worked together in silence. Over the past few weeks, he'd worked with Ezra long enough that he was able to do more than just hand tools to Ezra but was able to grab tools and use them himself.

"Would you mind if I ask for your advice on something?" he asked as they finished up, standing back to look at the job and make sure that there wasn't anything they had missed.

"You can go ahead and ask, but I can't guarantee that I'm going to say anything worth listening to."

Ezra was always so humble. Everyone respected his opinion and thought he was wise beyond words, and yet it didn't go to his head, and he didn't act like everyone should stand around and hang on his every word. It was one of the things that made him easy to listen to, at least in Cooper's eyes.

"I don't know how much you know about my past," he began.

"I think everyone knows you were a big singer. Famous. And had a lot of hit songs. Mina has even said that you were a heartthrob according to some of her classmates."

Cooper scoffed at that. "Hardly." He had never, not even once, thought of himself as a heartthrob. He wanted his music to mean something to people, but he definitely didn't want to become a sex symbol. Not even a little bit.

"Well, I guess I'm kind of famous. And part of the reason I'm here is because it got to be too much. Something bad happened, and the negative press and the way people lied about me drove me out of the spotlight. I just couldn't take the fact that the person who had done wrong to me went unpunished, while everyone considered me to be the bad guy. It offended my sense of right and wrong."

"I totally get that. I have a very strong sense of things needing to be right, and when they're not, I want to make them right. Lying is one of those things that just burns me to my bones. I hate it with passion."

"Yeah. I can't say I've never lied, but I've never lied to anyone like that, and I've never lied that publicly. And I've never lied and allowed someone else to pay for crimes I actually committed."

"That's all good. I'm happy about that. I hate to think you're the kind of person who would go around lying about people, trying to get them to pay for your crimes."

Ezra's words were a little ironic, and Cooper laughed.

"I know. I'm tooting my own horn. Sorry. I just wanted you to know what the problem was. I'm out of the spotlight for a reason."

"I understand. I don't think humans were designed to have that kind of spotlight on them. No one can stand to have that kind of scrutiny on their lives."

Cooper had never even considered that before. It had been something that had come with his fame, and he had accepted it as something he had to live with. But the idea that a human wasn't supposed to, and couldn't, had never crossed his mind. He tucked that idea away to think about later.

"Anyway. An opportunity has come up for me to use my name to help someone who has been a blessing to me. To return the favor, so to speak."

Ezra straightened, his arms crossed over his chest, leaning against the back of the side-by-side, his dark eyes giving nothing away.

"But doing that would mean that I would have to put myself back out in the spotlight. When I worked so hard these past six weeks to...not hide, but heal."

"I think there was some healing that was necessary. How are you feeling?" Ezra asked.

"I was thinking a couple of days ago how good I felt. I...feel like this is one of the best decisions I've ever made. You guys have been awesome. You could have taken my picture a million times and put it up in places where people would have known where I was, and been in touch with anyone who was trying to dig and find out what was going on, but no one has."

"I'm glad to hear that everyone's been considerate of your privacy and of your well-being," Ezra said casually, like he wasn't the one who had given the order that Cooper was strictly off-limits.

"I guess I just wanted to know your thoughts on that. Most of me wants to just stay here and hide out. But there's a part of me that wants to give back. And that's one way that I can."

"Can you find a way to give back that doesn't involve giving up what you've worked for?"

"I probably could, but I know that this way would be the perfect opening."

"Kind of like an opportunity that just presented itself to you, and it's so perfect you're tempted to take advantage of it?" Ezra asked, like he knew what he was talking about.

"Exactly."

Ezra was quiet for a moment, and then he said casually, "I don't believe in coincidences. If God has presented an opportunity for you to do something kind, I wouldn't count the cost. I'd just do the kindness. I don't think kindness and generosity are ever wasted. Ever. That's just my personal opinion though. The Bible says, 'As we have therefore opportunity, let us do good unto all *men*, especially unto them who are of the household of faith.'"

He had never thought of the verse that way before.

"And God also says that you can't outgive Him, and He promises that when you give, He'll give back to you pressed down, shaken together overflowing, and He'll have men give back to you. I was told that verse meant that God will inspire men to give back to you everything you've given and a lot more; it's a material thing. Although, I do believe that God will give us even more than anything we've ever given when we get to heaven. So, I suppose both interpretations are equally encouraging."

Cooper didn't need any more proof. He should definitely help Priscilla. Now, he just needed to set aside his natural reluctance to get back out where so much hurt had happened.

Chapter Fourteen

"Do you need me to grab anything from the grocery store?" Priscilla asked Alaska as she stood in the kitchen. Alaska had promised the kids that they were going to make bread today, and Justin and Zaylee were over the moon with excitement.

In Priscilla's experience, making bread was an exhausting experience, but she didn't talk about anything with her kids except how good it tasted. They didn't realize the hours of work that stood between a person and their food when it came to making bread.

"I think I'm good. Ada was just in yesterday and grabbed some things for me."

"I thought she'd be here helping today," Priscilla said as Alaska grabbed a sack of flour and instructed all of the children to wash their hands at the sink.

"She planned on it, but we had a cow down in the field. I think she had expelled her uterus. Ada is out there with the vet right now, since none of the guys had time to stop and help."

Priscilla nodded. She knew how it was; there was always something going on. And they were always stretched trying to figure out who could cover what. She was pretty sure she saw the farrier's truck down at the barn, and that meant he was there, and someone had to be with him as well. Plus, they had dude ranch visitors, and they were also trying to get some of the fall work done.

Priscilla's phone rang, and she grabbed it, swiping and putting it to her ear as she helped Zaylee finish washing her hands at the sink.

"Hello?"

"Hey, Priscilla. I'm out here in the field with a cow, and the vet's here, and I just remembered I was supposed to go sit with Jim today. Would you by any chance—"

Priscilla hesitated for a moment. She was supposed to get the groceries and deliver them to Cooper, but it would be a lot easier for her to postpone that than it would be for Ada to try to get away.

"Sure. What time?"

Ada answered, and Priscilla looked at her watch. She could easily make it, with a little bit of time to spare, but when Ada said that she was supposed to be there for two hours, she realized she was going to have to call Cooper and let him know that things were going to be delayed.

"I really appreciate you doing this. I'm sorry. I just knew that Alaska had the kids, and she's probably elbow deep in bread by now. She can't stop."

"No. That's fine. And usually Justin and Zaylee really love to go to sit with Jim and run around their backyard. I don't get that, but it's true." They had an entire farm they could run around on, but for some reason, put a fence up around a small plot of ground, and her kids thought it was the most awesome thing.

"All right. I gotta go. Thanks."

She hung up and turned to Alaska. "That was Ada, and she was supposed to sit with Jim today. I told her I would, but will you be okay with the kids?"

"They're going to be fine." Alaska grinned. "I doubt the bread will be done for a few hours anyway."

Priscilla nodded, but she didn't say anything. Her kids would just have to find that out the hard way. "You can send them home when they're done. Just text me and let me know where they are."

"We'll see what's going on. I'll keep you in the loop."

Both of her kids were old enough to be home by themselves, and she didn't mind leaving them there, but she liked to keep tabs on what they were doing and where they were, of course.

She told her kids she'd see them later and walked out the door, dialing Cooper's number. She didn't call him very often. More often than not, they exchanged terse text messages. Nothing beyond a few directions and times, and she saw that as a good thing.

She probably could have texted him, but she wanted to explain why she was going to be late, so he didn't feel like he was being bothered. For some reason, it bothered her that he might think that way.

"Priscilla?" Cooper answered.

Priscilla smiled. His greeting sounded concerned.

"Everything is okay." She wanted to reassure him immediately, since he sounded worried. "I just wanted to let you know that I'm going to be a little bit late with your groceries. Ada was supposed to sit with Agathe's husband, Jim, but she can't make it. So I said I would do it."

"You're going by yourself?" he asked, like he thought there might be some problem with that.

"Yes. Jim is harmless. He'll probably sleep the whole time I'm there anyway." She had plenty of books on her Kindle app. Although she usually kept a paperback book with her too, so she wouldn't run out of things to do when something like this came up.

"Sometimes people with dementia can be unpredictable."

"Jim is benign. Sometimes he gets lost, but that's the most concerning thing about him."

"Would you mind if I go with you?" he asked, and Priscilla blinked as she paused at the bottom of the porch steps.

"I would hate to put you out like that."

"You wouldn't be putting me out at all."

"You would have to drive into town. I'm sure you weren't planning on that today."

"I haven't been out of the house all day. I had a few things I needed to work on around here, and I wanted to rearrange my cupboard so I could have room for the groceries you were going to bring. But that all can wait."

"All right. If you insist." She wasn't going to argue with him if he wanted to come. To be honest, she wouldn't mind the company. If Jim wasn't in a talking mood, it wasn't hard, but sometimes if he were in an anxious time of day, she worried a bit about calming him down. That only happened a couple of times. Usually he was content to sleep in front of the TV.

"Do you know where they live?" she asked.

"Yeah. The kids showed it to me the last time I went to church. I can be there in about thirty minutes."

"All right. I'll be there by then, and I'll let you in."

They hung up, with Priscilla somehow feeling a lot lighter and a good bit more excited to see Jim than she had when Ada had asked her to take over.

She tried to tell herself that it wasn't because she was going to get to see Cooper. But she knew that was a lie. She'd been looking forward to seeing Cooper every time she went to his cabin for the last few weeks. Maybe even before that. He just... She wasn't sure what it was, but she enjoyed talking with him, enjoyed their conversations, and he not only made her laugh, but he was fun to be around and was able to converse on a wide range of topics, which she enjoyed.

Smiling to herself, she backed out and drove into town. After talking with Agathe for a couple of minutes, who told her that Jim had mostly been sleeping in his recliner since lunch, and she didn't anticipate him needing anything, Agathe left and Priscilla sat down at the kitchen table, pulling her phone out and getting a book up to read.

She was waiting for it to load when Jim shuffled out.

"Where's my wife? You're not my wife? You don't belong here!"

Priscilla's eyes widened. A couple of times, Jim had not recognized her, but he'd been really benign, affable, and they chatted for a bit before he dozed off in his chair.

Agathe had mentioned that she felt like she had to soon put Jim into a home. There were things that she had been unable to do and times where Jim refused to cooperate and got a little aggressive.

Since Priscilla had never seen it, she hadn't worried too much about it, but she realized that it might have been a warning for her that it could happen while she was there.

She couldn't believe she had totally missed it.

"I'm a friend of your wife's. She's gone to do some errands, and I'm staying here."

"What's your name?" Jim said, not looking very happy.

"Priscilla Clybourn."

The man's brows drew down even more. "I don't know of any Clybourns around these parts. And I've been here all my life. I think you're lying. What are you trying to steal?"

Priscilla didn't know how to answer that, although she tried to keep her voice modulated and speak in a soothing tone. "I promise I'm not trying to steal anything. Would you like to look through my purse?" She didn't know what else to offer.

Jim actually started to take a step forward, with his hand out, when there was a knock at the door.

"We better get that," Priscilla said, slowly pushing back away from the table and not wanting to admit how much relief flooded her body. She had been scared.

"Are you expecting company? It would be nice to have a visitor." Jim spoke in a soft tone, and it was like he had never accused her of stealing.

"Yes. It would, wouldn't it?" she asked, hurrying to the door and opening it up.

Cooper stood on the other side, and not just Cooper, but he was holding his guitar.

She didn't know what he read on her face, but she supposed there was relief, huge and expressive, there.

His eyes twitched, and then he looked at Jim before he looked back at her.

"Hey there," he said to her and then dipped his head at Jim.

"I'm so glad you're here," she said, knowing that her voice sounded a little breathy. "Come on in." She opened the door wider, and Cooper stepped in.

"You have a guitar," Jim said, not even mentioning that he didn't recognize Cooper.

"Yeah. I thought maybe we might like to sing a bit."

"That would be good," Jim said, and Priscilla tried to ignore her shaking legs.

"I don't know if you've met Cooper Cordray." She motioned to

Cooper. "Cooper, this is Jim. He's my neighbor and friend." Would Jim go along with that? Had he completely forgotten the allegations that he'd leveled against her just a few minutes prior?

"She was trying to steal stuff. She doesn't belong here. Her last name was some kind of name I don't recognize. I've lived in these parts for all my life. I would recognize her name if she was from around here. You better watch your pockets," Jim said, like he would like to kick the thief out of his house, as he turned and started shuffling toward the living room.

They already had the TV muted, although the picture blinked and flashed. Priscilla grabbed the remote and turned it off when they walked in.

Jim didn't seem to notice.

"What did you say your name was?" Jim asked Cooper, and Priscilla held her breath. Maybe he was going to say that he didn't recognize Cooper either. Maybe he'd try to throw them both out. Although, he was settling himself back down on his recliner.

"Cooper Cordray," Cooper said, and his voice sounded cautious, like his mind was going in the same direction as Priscilla's.

Jim's face scrunched up. "That sounds familiar. You live north or south of town?"

"Southeast," Cooper said, and his eyes twinkled as they met Priscilla's.

Maybe Jim recognized his name because he was so famous. That was hardly fair. Priscilla wanted to cross her arms over her chest and pout. She had lived in Sweet Water far longer than Cooper, but because he was famous, Jim gave him a pass?

She couldn't wait to tease Cooper about it.

"Oh yeah. I think I remember your family. Good stock."

"Musical people too. I'm told I'm not bad at the guitar, and I have a fair singing voice as well," Cooper said as he set his guitar case down, clapped open the latches, and pulled the instrument out.

He handled it with the confidence of someone who knew what they were doing, as Priscilla assumed he did.

She stood in the doorway, watching as Cooper sat down on a chair across from Jim.

"Is there something in particular you'd like to hear?"

"You choose. I'll think about it," Jim said after a bit of a pause.

Cooper glanced at Priscilla, and then he strummed a few chords on his guitar and launched into a song that sounded faintly familiar to her. Maybe one of his popular hits?

It didn't escape Priscilla's awareness that there were millions of people who would love to be in a position where she was right now, getting a personal concert from the world's biggest music superstar, but Cooper didn't act that way, and the room felt very cozy and casual and relaxed.

His voice was mellow, smooth, and absolutely perfect. She could see why millions of people loved it. It curled around her inside and slipped like velvet up and down her backbone.

She closed her eyes. What beautiful music.

The song faded away, and she opened her eyes, finding Cooper looking at her.

She was slightly embarrassed. He would know she had been enjoying his music, but surely he wouldn't be surprised. Lots of people did. It did not make her unique.

"That was nice. It sounded faintly familiar, but I don't really know it. You need to play something I know."

"All right. What do you know?" Cooper asked, not seeming the slightest bit insulted that someone had just told him that his voice, beloved around the globe, was okay. Nice.

"What about a hymn?" Jim said, after a small pause. He definitely was taking this whole picking his own song thing seriously.

Or else he was getting sleepy. Priscilla kind of hoped that was the case.

She decided she would walk in and sit down. There was no need for her to lurk in the doorway, and it wasn't Cooper's job to watch Jim, so she hated to leave them alone. Plus, she was getting treated to a concert, and she didn't want to listen from the other room.

"What would you like?" Cooper asked, and Priscilla was slightly surprised. She hadn't thought he would even know any hymns, let alone ask Jim to name one for him.

Jim seemed to be deep in thought, and after a few minutes, Cooper said, "Why don't you think about it, and I will see what Priscilla wants."

He looked over at her, and the words to a hymn she'd been thinking of came easily to her lips.

"A Thousand Tongues? The Charles Wesley hymn." It seemed to fit since he made his living singing.

He nodded. "That's a good one." Then, after just a few moments' thought, he strummed a bit on his guitar and started singing.

O for a thousand tongues to sing
my great Redeemer's praise,
the glories of my God and King,
the triumphs of his grace!

He knew all the words, which amazed Priscilla.

She joined in with harmony, surprised at how well their voices blended together. That hymn always made her want to sing forever.

My gracious Master and my God,
assist me to proclaim,
to spread thro' all the earth abroad
the honors of your name.

It seemed Cooper was equally surprised, since he had been kinda staring into space, staring at the ground, maybe concentrating on the words or the music or whatever singers concentrated on when they sang, but his eyes lifted to hers, and something stretched between them that seemed to bind them together without moving them at all. Maybe that was what happened when people sang together. She always felt a little bit like that when her family sang. Which they often did around the campfire, and they had done for years in the evening when her parents were still alive.

Jesus! the name that charms our fears,
that bids our sorrows cease,
'tis music in the sinner's ears,
'tis life and health and peace.
He breaks the power of cancelled sin,
he sets the prisoner free;
his blood can make the foulest clean;
his blood availed for me.

She supposed as they all got older and started doing their own things, the singing in the evening had fallen a bit by the wayside. Now that she had her own children at home, maybe it was something she could pick up on. She had always loved doing it as a child. There was just something really special about singing together.

To God all glory, praise, and love
be now and ever given
by saints below and saints above,
the Church in earth and heaven.

Their voices blended on the last note and held it before it faded off.

Jim was nodding his head, his eyes closed. He finally opened them and said, "That was real nice. I like that."

His eyes closed again, and it was hard to tell whether he was awake or asleep.

Cooper studied Jim for a moment, and then he said, as though Jim were looking at him and they were having a conversation, "I just wrote this song not too long ago. I haven't sung it for anyone yet, but I thought maybe you would like it."

He started to sing, and Priscilla figured this was one of the songs that he had written while she had been around. He had confessed to her that he had had a little bit of inspiration when she wasn't around, but for the most part, the only time he was able to write was when he could look at her.

She realized even now he might be having words and melodies going through his head. He said it happened almost constantly when he was with her.

Did that make her special? She tried not to think about that any deeper, but her brain kept picking at it. Did he get inspired by anyone else? Or was it just her? How could she have not even thought of asking him that? It hadn't even occurred to her to think that maybe there was something unique about their interactions.

For her part, she'd never met anyone like him, and what she felt for Cooper was indeed unique. She certainly didn't feel this way about anyone else. And the way she felt when she was with him was unique as well.

For some reason, she didn't want to admit that.

What was she afraid of?

Then, she started listening to the words that Cooper was singing and found herself smiling. It was sweet and lyrical, and as he sang the chorus for the third time, she found herself naturally adding harmony.

He didn't seem to mind, although his brows lifted as she joined him, and then he smiled, his lips curving up, and just seemed to enjoy the moment. As she was doing. She wasn't quite sure what was happening to her, but she was absolutely positive that the country music superstar was not going to be staying in Sweet Water, North Dakota, for the foreseeable future. Although they did have an actress who was married to a rancher not far from there.

Priscilla had met her in church multiple times, and she was so unpretentious and unassuming that Priscilla would have had no idea that she was a big star, if someone hadn't told her.

That was how Cooper was. He just was humble and unpretentious. It was something she really loved about him.

Liked. Something she liked about him. There was no love involved.

She just needed to remember that. Because she was afraid she was very close to forgetting.

Chapter Fifteen

Cooper set his guitar down. He'd been singing with Priscilla for more than an hour, and the time had flown by so quickly he hadn't even noticed. He always enjoyed singing, but singing with Priscilla had been different. Better. Far better. It wasn't just because their voices blended naturally, although that had been a surprise and something that had made his heart warm and spread the good feeling all over. It wasn't often that he found someone who matched him so well.

But Jim had been snoring for a while now, and Priscilla had motioned that maybe they should tiptoe out of the room.

He carefully placed his guitar in the case and latched it up. He didn't know how long he was going to be gone, but the guitar had been a last-second decision, and he was glad he had made it. Jim had definitely enjoyed it, but Cooper had enjoyed it more. For some reason, when he was around Priscilla, all he thought about was getting his songs written, and it didn't even occur to him to try singing with her.

What was it about Priscilla that just seemed to suit every part of him? And would it be possible that she could feel something too? He doubted it. It seemed like those kinds of things were never mutual.

You'll never know unless you say something.

He knew that. But did he even want to ask? After all, asking would, depending on her answer, open up the door to the idea that they might be open to a relationship. And he had sworn that was a no. Especially when it came to music. After everything he had been through, he would have thought that he would have learned. But here he was, contemplating the whole idea of falling again.

Of course, Regina Blue was supposed to be a professional relationship, and Priscilla wasn't anything close. Her voice blended beautifully with his, but he knew without asking that she would never be interested in leaving the farm to sing, and so he knew that was out.

"That guitar was a great idea," Priscilla said, her voice low as they moved to the kitchen and sat down at the table. He set the guitar against the wall, where he would be sure to see it when he left. He didn't want to forget it, and he definitely didn't want anything to happen to it. Not that he couldn't get another one, but it would take some doing, since there were no music stores anywhere near the Sweet View Ranch.

"It was just a spur-of-the-moment thing. But I guess it is pretty amazing what music does to people, isn't it?"

Jim had been the most soothed by the hymns that they had sung. Although, he had seemed to recognize some of Cooper's songs and had definitely liked a few of his newer ones.

"The new songs were the ones that you've written while you were here?"

He felt his cheeks wanting to burn red and was grateful that he had enough stubble to hide that. Although, his neck definitely felt hot.

"Yeah. All of them. And you guys were the first to hear them. I haven't played them even for my agent."

"Why not? They sounded amazing. Very professional and catchy."

Thankfully she acted like she didn't notice how romantic the songs were. She might not realize that that was part of her muse. How she inspired the romance that moved his heart and soul.

It was definitely a deeper connection than he ever felt with anyone, and she didn't even know it.

"I don't know. I have five or six fully ready songs and ten total that I've written, but I've just been holding off on them." He paused for a moment, not wanting to spoil the way the afternoon had been going. "I guess maybe after having everything stolen from me… I know I can trust my agent. I know I can trust people. But it's just hard to."

She nodded, and then her head tilted to the side. "But you trust me."

It seemed almost like a question, although it didn't sound like it.

She had figured out each song and was able to sing the chorus in harmony with him each time, and he supposed if she wanted to, she could steal them.

Somehow, the idea didn't scare him. Not even a little bit. He just knew that Priscilla wasn't that kind of person, and she wasn't going to be taking anything from him that wasn't hers.

Are you really sure?

He admitted he had no fear, but maybe it was his brain telling him he still couldn't be sure.

"I guess I do. To some extent. I suppose after something like that happens to someone, you have a hard time rationalizing anything. Because your gut instinct is to clench everything tight to you and never trust again."

"I know you're right."

Her words were said simply, but they reminded him that she had also been hurt very badly by someone who had broken promises to her, and had paid dearly for it. She knew exactly what he was talking about.

Maybe they would both have the same issues. Maybe she really did feel something for him but didn't want to act on it, because she was the same way he was. Not wanting to trust someone again. For some reason, that thought started another one. It wasn't fair. It wasn't fair for her to blame him or make him pay for what her ex-husband had done.

He wanted to argue his case immediately, but they weren't even talking. Not about the two of them together anyway.

"Jim and Agathe have been married for decades. He was stationed in Europe when they met and fell in love. She left her home country of France and has lived here ever since."

"That would be really hard to leave your home country."

"I know, right? And North Dakota does not exactly have the same kind of climate as France."

"Hardly. Nor the same scenery."

"No. Which is nice if you're visiting, but if you're moving to somewhere completely unfamiliar, and nothing is comfortable, it would be even harder. But she loved him."

He smiled. One of the lines in his song talked about a woman loving and following her love wherever he went.

"So they're like the song," he said, still wondering if she had made any connections between her and words that he had written. Wondering how he would explain it if she asked him about it. He had no idea.

"Yes. I suppose. But I often wonder if maybe we confuse the love that we expect a woman and a man to have together with the kind of love that we are supposed to have for the Lord. Because aren't we supposed to follow Jesus wherever he leads? Aren't we supposed to give our lives to Him? And yet, we try to fill that up with romantic love, and it makes us feel all gushy and happy inside, but... I'm not sure that's the way it was supposed to be."

He paused. Her mind had gone in a completely different direction, and as usual, she was thinking about things that he had never thought about before in his life. The idea that the world's love was not the right kind of love.

"You're saying that we basically make our spouses as gods and break the first commandment?"

"I don't know about that. I guess I wouldn't go that far. But I do think sometimes we expect 'love,'" she used air quotes, "to be more than what it actually is. At least between two humans. Because I think everyone wants someone to admire them and to respect them and to think they're amazing. And yet God already does that for us, and that doesn't satisfy us. We're looking for a human to do that. And we're looking for a human to give our admiration and respect and all of our good thoughts toward. Yet, we're commanded in the Bible to put God first. To love Him, to respect Him, and to think about Him all the time. I guess, it seems a little suspect to me anyway."

"Do you think that's where you went wrong with your first marriage?" he asked, and then he wished he wouldn't have said that. He didn't mean to bring up bad memories or to hit her when she didn't deserve it.

But she didn't take it wrong at all. In fact, he was surprised at her answer.

"I've wondered about that. Did I? Is that where I made the mistake? Did I think that my husband was going to love me and cherish me, which he was supposed to do, and I never really paid attention to what God wanted to do? That He wanted to love and be loved by me? I never even acknowledged all the things that God did for me out of His great love for me. I just...wonder sometimes if I've been wrong all this time."

He noticed that she wasn't accusing anyone of being wrong. She was just stating her thoughts.

"But the way you think, the way you believe comes from what you were taught. And it's not so much you being wrong as the church not teaching us the right way to love God and the right expectations to have for our spouses." He had never really thought about that before, but as he was teasing it out of his brain, that's what came out.

"I think I might have to look up some verses and make sure that I agree with you. But I think you might be right. We've been told that God is love and that He loves us, no matter what we do. I think we have a tendency to apply that toward sin. God loves us even if we sin. God loves us if we do this or that, so we don't have to worry about it, because God's not going to judge us. And that's what people sometimes take away. That God really doesn't care, when I believe He does."

"I believe He does too. Otherwise, He wouldn't have had to send Jesus to die. I don't know if that is necessarily even a matter of Him caring as much as it's a matter of fact. It's just like gravity. We can't stop it, we can't change it. And we have to follow the law. The Bible says God is holy, and He wants us to be holy too. So just because He loves us even though we sin doesn't mean we should just go ahead and sin and not care."

"I agree," she said simply.

They didn't say anything for a moment, and there were a million thoughts going through his head. Yes, God wanted them to be holy, but God was also love. And He wanted them to love as He had loved. Which probably went hand in hand with being holy. Because most sins were against other people, and if you loved them, you wouldn't sin against them by lying to them or cheating on them or dishonoring their bodies by committing fornication with them.

It wasn't just about what a person didn't do. It was about what a person did. The kindness and generosity that a person showed when they truly loved someone the way God loved them. After all, God was the most generous being ever. It was impossible to outgive the Lord, whether in physical things or in something more abstract, like love.

And that was when he thought about what it was that he could do for Priscilla and how she hadn't even asked, hadn't mentioned it, hadn't suggested it.

Had the thought even crossed her mind?

"I know this is a big change in the subject, but how is your social media account doing? Are you making more money with it?"

"It's about the same." She lifted her shoulder, like it didn't matter. "I know we always hear about people going viral, but I think this is the same as anything else. People who go viral are usually the people who've been working on it for a long time. Every day, day in and day out, doing the same thing, doing the work, because after all, luck can't strike if you're not in a position for it."

"A lot of people think that I just got lucky with my singing. But it's like you said. I spent a lot of time playing my guitar when everyone else was out playing with their friends, I spent time singing and being the entertainment when everyone else was being entertained."

"You were working when everyone else was playing."

She didn't ask, but he nodded anyway. "That's exactly right. I agree with you that a lot of people think that it should be easy to be successful, but it's just not. It requires a lot of work and sacrifice." But that wasn't what he had been thinking about. She always turned things back on him and made him look good. "How long have you been working on it?"

She knew exactly what he was talking about. "Just six months. Maybe a little longer. I didn't start when I should have. I guess I was too busy being sad and depressed about not having my children. I didn't really work on anything other than wanting to get them back." She pressed her lips together, and then her hand traced along the edge of the table. "I think I wasted a lot of time worrying about stuff I had no control over. I couldn't change any of it, other than continue to look for a job in Wyoming that would support me and the children. I knew there was no point in me just going back, because while I would have been able to see my kids, I wouldn't have been able to have a job where I would have made enough money to be granted full custody. And God had a plan all along. I just didn't see it. And instead of me working on something, building something, I just sat around and worried. Sat around and was angry that I didn't have what I wanted. Sat around and questioned God and demanded that He do what I wanted Him to do. I'm embarrassed about it now, but at the time, I felt like I was right and He was wrong."

She laughed a little. And then she looked embarrassed.

"Isn't that crazy? I thought God didn't know what He was doing. I thought He wasn't in control of things. I thought He was letting other people get things that I wasn't able to have, and I was jealous and upset. How ridiculous could I possibly be?" Her head shook, and she tapped on the table.

"I wouldn't give yourself too hard a time about it. I have done the same thing." Just recently. Just with his latest thing with Regina Blue, he was so angry and upset and held it against everyone, but... If it hadn't been for Regina Blue, he wouldn't be sitting here right now, and he wouldn't have the five or so full songs that he had just written. The best songs of his career, he was almost certain. He wouldn't know this amazing woman, the one who tempted him to trust again and made him desire a wife and family. Who inspired him on an almost daily basis and was responsible for the rebirth of his creativity.

"I found that a lot of times, the things we think are terrible are actually good."

"I've heard you say that before, and I disagreed, but I was actually just sitting here right now thinking that maybe the thing that I thought was the worst thing that ever happened to me in my life will turn out to be the best."

"Really?" she asked, looking interested. Could he share?

"Yeah. You know the woman who had been touring with me and I wrote songs. Kinda of the same way I've been doing with you, only she was not my muse the way you are. She was just there while I was writing and heard me sing the lyrics and work out the melody. I didn't know that she was writing down everything I was, taking the songs that I was creating, and eventually she said they were hers."

"But she was there. Wasn't she writing the songs too?"

He shook his head. "She never gave any suggestions. She was just in close proximity and spent time with me. We...were a couple at one point."

He hesitated to admit that. But she nodded, like she had already known it. It wasn't something that got around, although people had linked them romantically for a while. It was hard to spend that kind of time with someone and not feel an attraction and a bit of a crush on them. But then, as a person spent more time with someone, their true colors came out. Although, in most cases, Cooper believed that a person's bad qualities were not so large that they couldn't be overcome. However, with Regina Blue, that was not true, since her bad qualities included cheating and stealing.

"Anyway, I did all the writing. I'd sing to her, and she might say 'oh yeah, that was good' or 'that's just not quite ready,' but it wasn't like she was giving suggestions and helping with the song. More often than not, I just sang what I had. She listened to me, yes. She gave me advice, yes. She gave me her opinion, all the time." He hoped he was explaining it right. Because the songs were his. "It would be like someone writing a book and reading part of the book and having someone say 'maybe you should take that line out' or 'I don't like this part of it.' They didn't write the book. They didn't come up with the ideas."

"I totally get it. She lied."

"Yeah. That was probably the worst part. Not only did she steal the songs from me, but she claimed that I tried to steal them from her. My own songs."

"I'm shocked that you're singing songs for me. That you're even discussing it with me."

"I resisted at first. A lot." He took a deep breath and looked through the living room doorway, where he could barely see Jim's feet on the recliner. The man hadn't moved. "For that very reason."

"So what changed your mind?" she asked, her head lifted, her eyes confused.

"I don't know. I guess... I hate to say I trusted you, because it sounds so trite. But obviously I did, since you're the only one who's heard the new songs I've written. Well, you and Jim," he said, looking back over at Jim's feet.

Priscilla nodded, a ghost of a smile on her face.

"I don't know. I guess I struggled with myself for a really long time, I went back and forth about whether I could or couldn't, and finally I decided that I would and I asked if I could write while you are around. I guess you just seem so supportive. You didn't seem interested in the actual song as much as you seemed interested in...me. And being kind to me. Encouraging and helpful, but not in the kind of way that made it seem like you were going to take anything from me."

"It probably helps that I can't sing."

"You have a fine voice."

"Well, I don't sing. I don't have a stage, I don't have an audience; there's no way I could do anything with your songs anyway."

He huffed out a laugh. "I had never even thought about that. Or at least, those weren't the thoughts foremost on my mind. I suppose when something like that happens to you, you're not always the most rational person about it."

She nodded, as though she understood, and he thought that maybe she did.

"What happened between you and your ex?" That seemed like a probing, personal question, but if it was what he suspected...

"He cheated on me." Her words were soft, but they were clipped. It made the case open and closed. She didn't need to give details. Someone who would cheat was a scumbag who didn't deserve to have a family and certainly didn't deserve a woman like Priscilla.

"And you find it hard to trust again?"

She nodded. "I don't plan to ever get married again. I don't know how I would ever trust someone. After all, my ex was a clean-cut, upstanding, bright guy; my parents approved, my brothers approved, my whole family loved him. No one ever saw it coming." She paused for a bit. "I suppose, more than anything else, I wondered what I did wrong. What did I do to make him cheat? Why wasn't I the kind of wife who could keep his interest?"

"It wasn't you." He wasn't there. He really didn't know, but he could tell for sure that it didn't matter what she did, a man should stay true to his word.

"I know. It took me a long time to come to that conclusion. I struggled for a long time thinking that it was my fault somehow. I suppose it didn't help that he told me it was."

"He's a jerk. If he can't stay true to his wife, it's not your fault." His words were said with a lot more force than strictly necessary, but it was absolutely true.

"I know." She smiled a little, almost as though she was laughing at his anger. He realized how silly he was being and forced himself to take a deep breath and blow it all out. "I figured it out. I'm okay."

Was that what she had found so funny? That he obviously cared about her, because he was coming to her defense.

"You've just been so good to me. I hate the idea of some man treating you badly. You don't deserve that."

"I don't know that I necessarily do or don't deserve things. I wasn't a perfect wife. I just wasn't. Because there is no such thing. Not because there's anything wrong with me. And I guess I figured that out. I would never be a perfect wife. As hard as I might try, as many things as I might try to fix, I wasn't going to be perfect. He had to have the character to stay. He had to have the character to choose to do the hard things. I couldn't make him do that." She shrugged her shoulders again. "I appreciate your defense, though I didn't need it for the most part."

His hand sat on the table, and he realized it was just a hair's breath away from hers. He moved slightly and touched her finger with his.

"I'm glad. I wish you wouldn't have had to go through it to begin with."

"And I guess we're back to what we were talking about before. Going through that made me a better person. It showed me some of the things I was doing wrong. I just said, I wasn't a perfect wife. I saw some areas where I could improve. Not just as a wife, but as a person. And maybe I wouldn't be back here now. Here in North Dakota with my whole family. I'm happy." She shrugged her shoulders, but her eyes were glowing. "My kids are with their cousins every day. I'm homeschooling, for goodness' sake. I never thought that would happen."

"You do a lot of work."

"I love the work. I love cleaning your house and shopping for groceries and being in charge of our other rental guests, doing the towels and linens, folding them. There's something so pleasurable about folding sheets and pillowcases and towels. It's not hard work, it's just... really easy work where I can sit and think about how much Jesus loves me. I know that sounds trite, but the more I think about how much He loves me, the more I seem to be able to love others. It's a weird thing, but true."

He had never thought about that before. He knew God loved him, something that every kid was taught in Sunday school, but had he really understood exactly how much? Did he consider if there was more to it than what he knew?

But somehow, the idea of thinking about God's love reminded him that he could do something for this woman who sat in front of him.

But before he could say anything, she said, "You should write a song to sing for our family Thanksgiving get-together program. All the cousins that are homeschooled put on their things that they've been working on. It gives them an audience to perform for, and it gives us an excuse to get together and eat."

He laughed. "Will I be the only adult performing?" He didn't know why that mattered. A lot of times, he was the only adult performing. If he didn't have an opening act.

"Does that matter?" she asked, as though she could read his mind.

"I guess it doesn't. But maybe I should say this, I'll do it, as long as you do it with me."

"Are you serious?" she asked, sounding totally shocked. "You are the big superstar singer, and you're not going to sing unless me, somebody who is nobody in the singing world, sings with you?"

"You might be nobody in the singing world, but I'm nobody in your family. So, having you beside me gives me credibility."

She shook her head, laughed, and then said, "All right. I'll sing, but I'd like to practice a lot beforehand. I know it's just my family, and they'll love anything we do, but it's been years since I've had to get up and do anything."

"You used to have to get up in front of people?"

"When I was homeschooled myself. That's what Mom did. Our family was our audience. I mean, there's twelve of us kids, plus Mom and Dad, so there were a lot of people. We had a song or a piece of poetry that we'd memorize, or an instrumental piece. Whatever it was, the rest of the family was our audience, and we had to get up and perform."

"Not every homeschooling family has that, but I guess it was really nice for you."

"Probably. But kids can be brutal, and siblings can be even worse, so the nerves were real." She laughed a little, and he got the feeling that it wasn't that bad.

"Thanks for the warning."

"They're a lot better than they used to be. In fact, all of them are encouraging now. But you know how you have these memories and they affect what you do."

"Yeah. I know all about that." And he really did. The memories of Regina Blue and her betrayal affected everything that he had done with Priscilla. How he hadn't trusted her, how he hadn't offered to help her, how he hadn't treated her as well as she had been treating him.

He was trying to figure out how to ask her if she'd like for him to make a guest appearance on one of her videos when the door opened and Agathe walked in.

His opportunity had passed for now, but he'd keep an eye out for it later. He owed Priscilla that much.

Chapter Sixteen

"I don't know if I can do this," Justin said, standing at the side of the bunkhouse, looking over the people who were assembled. They were his aunts and uncles and cousins and friends and family, other than Cooper, who definitely qualified as a friend. At least Priscilla qualified him in that way.

"Of course you can do it. These are people who love you. Everyone's going to be encouraging you."

"Zaylee's going to make fun of me," he said, sounding annoyed.

"No, she's not."

"Alice said that she couldn't wait to hear me," Zaylee said, talking about Ezra and Alaska's oldest daughter.

"I'm sure she can't. She's going to love what you're doing."

"And Mina said that she thought Justin was going to do a really good job."

Mina was a young girl who spent a lot of time with Bo and Claudia Hansen. Claudia married their neighbor Bo, and while they didn't have any children of their own, some of those cousins were sitting in the audience.

Rohan and Aaron—the children of her twin sister, Phoebe, and her husband, Tillman—were about her own kids' age, and they were over on the side getting ready as well.

She looked around at all of the little ones coming up, the babies who kept multiplying, the moms who either had just had babies or were soon to have them, and then at her siblings who weren't even married yet—Ada helped Phoebe with her children, and Lois, her other unmarried sister, was around somewhere.

Rufus, her only brother who wasn't married, had spent most of the day making the stage. They had never had much of a stage before, but Rufus had been working on it off and on and finally finished up that morning.

She had to admit, Rufus had done an excellent job on it.

She smiled, when she thought back to the first days where her mom had made them stand up in front of all their younger siblings and do the recitations. They'd come a long way since then.

"I don't know why I'm so nervous," Cooper came over and said, his voice low, and she supposed she was probably the only one who could hear him. Other than her children.

"You're nervous?" Justin asked, raising his brows.

Cooper nodded, lifting his shoulder. "I haven't been this nervous since I can't remember when."

"But you sing in front of thousands of people!" Justin said.

Cooper smiled. "I know. You'd think that I would be used to this, but maybe it's because I usually have musicians and other people around me, and today it's just going to be me and my guitar."

Priscilla didn't believe that was it. After all, Cooper played lots of places with just him and his guitar.

"I think it's more that sometimes it's harder to do things in front of people you know and love, because you're afraid that they'll be disappointed in you. It is easier to do things in front of complete strangers, because you don't always care what the strangers think."

For some reason, Cooper looked at Priscilla when he said that, and she felt something twist and tighten her stomach. What was he trying to say? That he cared what she thought? She couldn't believe that.

"But isn't Mom going to sing with you?" Justin pointed out.

Cooper nodded. "Maybe that makes me more nervous, because if I mess up, it's going to affect her too."

"No. I'll be fine. If you mess up, I'll just go along with it, and we'll pretend that we meant to do it."

He smiled at her. "That's the kind of person I like to have standing beside me. Someone who's going to go down with the ship. And pretend we meant to do it."

She had to laugh at that. Obviously a shipwreck was not intentional, no matter how they swung it, and she assumed that's what he was trying to say.

Somehow, realizing that if she messed up, it would affect him, made butterflies start fluttering in her own stomach.

"You guys better go over and take your seats now. I'll be right here," she said. She gave them each a hug before they gave her tremulous smiles and moved to sit down with the other kids.

Ada was mostly in charge of the program, although she had not given anyone their assignments. Their respective moms had decided what the kids were going to do for the program, Ada was just coordinating it all.

Ezra got up and welcomed everyone to the evening, talking about the food that was available afterward and welcoming guests and family alike.

They always started with the youngest kids first, and the little ones got up on the stage and were as adorable as they could possibly be.

"It's like herding cats, but they're so sweet," Cooper said.

Priscilla nodded. "That age is so much fun. I mean, from birth to two is exceptionally hard work, but from two to five, I always really enjoyed."

"And after five, you're ready to send them back?" Cooper said with a laugh in his voice.

Priscilla chuckled under her breath. "No. I actually love this stage more, but I just haven't gone through it completely yet, so I didn't want to jinx anything."

"So this is your favorite age?"

"Yeah. By far. They're old enough to be independent. I don't have to have someone watching them constantly. I'm not afraid they'll kill themselves by doing something ridiculously dumb, and they're...not my friends exactly, but we can have conversations together, you know?"

They clapped as the little ones were done and headed back to their seats.

It was only an hour for the program. As the kids got older, and there were more of them, it would last longer, or else...they would quit doing it at all. The thought made Priscilla sad, but she understood that a lot of families didn't stay together as long as her family had to begin with. It was very unusual. So, it made sense that she had been blessed beyond words and needed to be grateful for her good fortune. To appreciate what the Lord had given her and to accept each day as it came, not looking into the future too hard, any harder than it would be to decide that she wanted to adjust the trajectory of her life.

"If I had a family like this, I wouldn't have wanted to ever leave it," Cooper said softly as Ada got up on the platform and announced that the children's part was over, but they had one last special thing.

"I have something I want to talk to you about later," Cooper said softly.

"All right," Priscilla said, thinking this was an awkward time for him to say that. Was he having a problem?

"It's nothing bad. I just wanted to make an offer, and I keep forgetting until we have something else to do, and then I can't."

"All right," she said. An offer. Did he want to buy his cabin? Did he want her to record a song with him? She recoiled at that idea. She could sing, but not well, and she definitely didn't want to hear her voice on the radio or anything like that. It would be too...weird. That wasn't where her calling was in life, of that she was sure.

Ezra said their names at that point, and Cooper took a look at her, and she returned his smile, nodding her head. She was ready, as ready as she would ever be.

"After you," Cooper said, putting a hand behind her back, allowing her to walk forward first.

At certain times, she was happy she was a woman, because the polite thing to do was to let the lady go first, but she wanted to hide behind Cooper at this point.

Still, she squared her shoulders and stepped up onstage, having performed in front of her family for so long that it almost felt like coming home to be up there. The only thing she was worried about was Cooper. She had never performed in front of him before. Not that she was performing, she was just singing harmony on the chorus.

They didn't have microphones, and they didn't have a stool either. Cooper had specifically said no when asked, because Priscilla hadn't wanted to sit down.

But they did stand side by side. And as Priscilla looked out over the crowd of people, all of them friends and family, all of them beloved by her, she felt such a wonderful sense of thankfulness and gratefulness for the community God had given her. The whole point of the celebration was for Thanksgiving, and it made sense that she would be feeling so grateful she could hardly express it. Grateful for all these people who provided her support when she needed it, who took care of her children, who gave her a place to stay and a job to do and wise counsel and made her feel safe and beloved, and who reminded her that God loved her and that He had a plan for her life.

She had seen that the worst thing she thought could happen to her had turned out for good, and part of the good was standing in front of her right now.

Maybe, maybe the song that Cooper and she were going to sing would be a little bit of a blessing to them.

Originally, they had said that they would sing one of the songs that Cooper had written, but it just seemed to make more sense for them to sing a song of thankfulness.

As he started to strum his guitar, Priscilla listened, smiling. By now, they'd practiced it at least ten times, and the introduction was familiar, and as Cooper's rich, mellow voice started to sing the words, it felt even more right.

Even though she had wanted to do a good job so she didn't embarrass him, she knew that no matter what she did, he wouldn't be upset. He just wasn't the kind of person who got concerned about those kinds of things. He laughed easily, and beyond the obvious trust issues he had because of the thing he had been through recently, he laughed easily and smiled often.

He was good with kids, and enjoyed helping on the farm, and got along with her siblings. To the point where he was actually standing up at her family Thanksgiving program and doing his own song.

Lots of times through the years, their friends and family had gotten together and performed at each other's programs, so it wasn't totally unusual to have someone who wasn't family onstage, but as she looked out over the people sitting there, their eyes glued on Cooper, little smiles on their faces as they listened to him sing the words, she figured that they'd never had someone of his caliber for sure.

It was her time to join in, and she sang softly, blending her voice with Cooper's but not overpowering his. Not that she could. His voice was rich and mellow, but he could project it quite easily when he needed to.

She felt the words and music the whole way to her soul and felt a contentment and a gratefulness swell deep inside of her. Hopefully it was the effect the song was having on everyone, because it was what she wanted to feel for this holiday. Gratefulness to the Lord for the goodness that He had done and the blessings that He had bestowed on her. More than she deserved, by far.

Her voice trailed off as Cooper started the second verse. He sang it just as well, and she came in on the chorus, and then he played a short solo on the guitar, and they sang the chorus again. Then it was over. That was it, but it had been an experience of a lifetime. Whether it was performing with Cooper, or just knowing how good God was, or a combination of the two of them, she wasn't sure, but she'd never had this deep, soul-encompassing feeling that she felt the whole way to her bones. As her family stood and clapped and smiled and cheered, she looked at Cooper, who had been looking at her, and smiled at him.

It wasn't planned, but he took her hand, raised it in the air, and then they bowed slightly together.

Then, as her family continued to clap, she turned and walked off the stage. They were calling for Cooper to do another song, and maybe he would, but she didn't have anything else ready and was more than willing to give the spotlight over to him.

"Aren't you going to sing anything else? Are you really going to just tease us like that? That was amazing," Ada said, standing below the stage and looking up at Cooper. Priscilla had already made her way off.

"I guess I can sing another one, if you really want me to, but this is your family's program. I don't want to take it over."

"You wouldn't be taking it over if you sang one more song. We promise we'll be content with that, right?" Ada turned and looked around. There were some grumbles, but for the most part, it looked like everyone would go along.

"All right then, if Priscilla will come back up here with me. We'll do one more."

Chapter Seventeen

"So you're halfway through your six-month self-imposed isolation. How's it going?" Bradley Fox asked Cooper as Cooper stood at the window in his cabin, looking out into the dark night. He was still on a glowing high from the evening that he'd spent with the Clybourns. And Priscilla. He was on the high from Priscilla.

"I don't think I said I was going to limit myself to six months. I'm pretty sure I said something along the lines of I thought six months was a good start."

"Really? I didn't think you'd make the full six months."

"Good to know you have faith in me," Cooper said, allowing humor to color his tone.

"You know what I mean," Bradley said and didn't explain anymore.

Cooper knew exactly what Bradley meant. Bradley was a good friend, he was his agent too, but a friend first. At least that's the way Cooper saw him, and he was pretty sure Bradley felt the same way.

"I was honestly thinking about never going back." There. He said what he'd been thinking for a while.

"Interesting. I was not expecting it, but I guess I can see why."

Cooper figured that was the way Bradley would react. He heard all the horror stories about agents pushing their clients to do all the things to make all of the money, and Bradley really had given him great, solid advice for years. But Bradley was always more concerned about him as a person, as a human being, than he was about him as a moneymaking machine. That was one of the things that made Bradley better than most agents in Cooper's opinion.

"Do you think you'd be happy?" Bradley's question was asked calmly, rationally, and Cooper knew he didn't have an agenda.

"I think so. I really can see myself never setting foot onstage again." Except for the family stage, where he would be with family, and that was the key word, "with," not "for" or "to." It felt like a big, close-knit group, which really made him want to be a part of it.

And not by himself. With Priscilla.

Was he really thinking that?

"I watched you over the past few years. Not just the debacle with Regina Blue, but the way you shot to fame and the way you seemed to handle it so well, but there always seemed to be a part of you that didn't really enjoy it."

Cooper appreciated Bradley's insight. "I guess I always thought of myself as a quiet, private person. It's impossible to have that kind of lifestyle with what I do. Everybody wants to know every single thing about you that they possibly can. And there's a part of me that wants to give that to them, you know? After all, they gave me my livelihood, and it was a really good one." He didn't know why he was talking in past tense. He hadn't quit anything, and he was still making money and could at any time. It wasn't like that part was gone. But he was thinking of walking away from it. He had plenty of money to support himself for the rest of his life and to leave huge endowments to his children...but he didn't have any children. And seeing the Clybourn family had made him think that maybe that wouldn't be such a bad thing.

Watching Priscilla with her children, seeing how much fun they had, how they interacted, how she loved them, how they made their little cabin feel so homey and happy. He loved going to her place, because he felt drawn into the warmth and vitality there. Unlike his, which still felt cold and impersonal, even though he'd lived there for three months.

"I want you to do what you think is best for you."

Those were big words coming from Bradley. After all, Cooper made up more than half of his income. But Bradley had gotten wealthy from Cooper's success as well.

"Maybe you're ready to slow down?"

Bradley laughed. "I don't think that's necessarily a bad idea. I wouldn't be against it. I don't have millions in the bank like you do, but I have enough. And while I love what I do, I love getting to help people, I guess I've been starting to think that maybe life is about more than being successful at my job and making a lot of money."

"Same." Except he loved to sing. He loved seeing people enjoy his songs, to be changed and improved and encouraged and whatever else his songs did for people. He just loved that.

Maybe that was the way Bradley loved helping people the way he did. It was a very similar thing.

"I guess when you know what you're doing, you can let me know."

"You're welcome to come out here. I know it's a little late to invite you out for Thanksgiving." Bradley had called to wish him a happy Thanksgiving since it was the next day.

"I'll be spending it with my family anyway."

They said a few more words before Cooper hung up with Bradley's words ringing in his ears. He said he would be spending it with his family. Cooper's grandma had long since passed, and he hadn't even called his family for the last few years over the holidays, let alone any other time. His sister had called him to ask if she could have tickets to one of his concerts so her kids could come. Then of course, he'd sent them, even meeting them backstage. It was like meeting strangers. His brother had never acknowledged his immense success, and he couldn't remember the last time he'd talked to him.

He probably still had his phone number. He could return home. But he figured that they probably would never be close. They lived in different states, and the more time Cooper spent in North Dakota, the more he thought that maybe he would stay.

Still, he had a longing to renew ties with his family.

Why not call his family? He lifted his phone up and searched through his contacts for his sister. She would be the easier one to call.

Glancing at his watch, he realized it was later than he thought and she might be in bed.

"Hello?" she answered after the fourth ring.

"Lynn. It's Cooper."

"That's what my phone said. But I had a hard time believing it. It's been so long since we talked."

He felt bad. She was right. He hadn't talked to her in a long time.

"I'm sorry. I've been...busy." He said the last word almost lamely. Everyone was busy. It was no excuse. He could make time for the things he wanted to make time for. Most of the time anyway. Sometimes there were actually times where his schedule wasn't his own.

"It's okay. It's good to hear your voice."

"It's good to hear you too. How are the kids?"

They chatted for a bit, and it wasn't as awkward as what he thought. He ended by wishing her a happy Thanksgiving and promising to not allow so much time to go by before he reached out again.

He hung up, feeling pretty good. He supposed he should have asked her about Gene, his brother. Could he call him?

He lived on the West Coast, so it wasn't as late for him, and Cooper decided he might as well. If he waited until tomorrow, he might not do it.

That conversation was a little bit more awkward with Gene really having no clue why he might have called and being suspicious that he might actually want something or be in trouble. He followed the news and knew that things hadn't always been peachy keen for Cooper over the last year. Still, by the time they were done, they wished each other a happy Thanksgiving and promised to keep in touch.

Cooper hung up the phone with an even better glow in his heart, if that were possible. Having the Thanksgiving program with the Clybourns, and with Priscilla in particular, couldn't be topped, but they'd inspired him to do something to make other people's lives better, and he felt amazing.

He took a deep breath, turning from the window and moving across the room to pick up his guitar. He had a song he'd been working on from the last time he'd been with Priscilla, and it was running through his mind now. She had changed his life, and not intentionally. Just by being her. She taught him to slow down, to look at the world through the eyes of Jesus, and to value the simple things, family and friends and doing things just to put a smile on someone's face.

He should probably thank her for that, but it was definitely too late to call. He'd see her tomorrow, since the Clybourns had invited him to Thanksgiving dinner and he had every intention of going. He was even going to take mashed potatoes. He smiled, thinking about the day ahead and wondering when the last time was that he had looked forward to a holiday with so much anticipation. Sure he hadn't done so since before his grandma died.

Chapter Eighteen

"Can we stay all night?" Justin asked with Zaylee standing beside him, a pleading look on both of their faces.

Priscilla looked down at her children. How could she say no to them?

She looked up to see Alaska looking at her and smiling. She nodded at the questioning look in Priscilla's eyes. She had already given her permission.

"You can stay, but I want you to be a help, and no fighting," Priscilla said. Part of her was sad that she would be spending Thanksgiving evening without her children, and part of her was beyond happy that her children had their cousins so close by, and they got along so well, and they wanted to spend so much time together.

They had just had a sleepover at Priscilla's house the week before, and Alaska's kids had been hoping they could return the favor.

Of course for her kids, it was always more exciting to go to someone else's house.

"It looks like it's just you and me for the walk home," Cooper said as he came up beside her in time to see her children cheering and hugging their cousins.

Snow was coming down, and it was still early enough in the season that everyone was excited about it. Especially since it came on Thanksgiving, and they had been able to enjoy watching it snow before it got dark.

"You guys better hurry up, there's already about three or four inches. If you're not careful, you'll have to shovel in order to get to your house," Alaska said, laughing.

"I'll be there to plow you guys out in the morning. Don't worry about coming over and feeding calves. Someone here will do it," Ezra said, coming over and putting his arm around his wife. She leaned into him, and Priscilla smiled. They had such an amazing relationship, and they seemed so happy with each other and together. There were always smiles and laughter. Being in their house always made her feel at home.

"If I can do anything, let me know," Cooper said.

Ezra nodded. "I'm sure eventually we'll have you out helping to push snow. It's a never-ending process in winter sometimes. But for now, enjoy your break." Ezra smiled, and then Priscilla hugged Alaska and they headed out.

"You don't have to walk me home. You could have left whenever you wanted to."

"I wanted to stay."

He didn't say anything more. Priscilla didn't doubt the sincerity of his words. He seemed to have a really good time, and he didn't exactly glow, but he seemed lighter somehow than he had when she first met him, and she figured that it was the effect of her family and the love and closeness that they all shared.

"Thank you. I don't mind walking home by myself, but it's always nicer to walk with someone."

"Especially in the snow," he said, looking around at the flakes falling down. "And I agree, it's always nicer to walk with someone, as long as it is the right someone."

She heard the wistful note in his voice and wondered at it. Maybe he just had been with the wrong someone at times, and that had affected him.

"Well, I'm glad that I'm on your enjoy walking home in a snowstorm list." She smiled and bumped him with her shoulder. She probably shouldn't have. She had been trying to keep a physical distance between them, since her thoughts seemed to constantly go to him, and when they were in the same room, she found herself gravitating toward him.

He was going to be leaving, and there was a part of her that wished it was sooner rather than later, since the longer he stayed, the more she felt the pull, and the harder she found it to stay away from him.

"I was thinking we could do that video tomorrow. The one we talked about, where I do it with you?"

She thought he'd forgotten. Or maybe reconsidered. She felt like it was a big sacrifice for him, since he was trying to lie low, and being in a video with her certainly was a major thing. Although, she only had around fifteen hundred followers, so it wasn't like he was going to be showing himself to the world.

"Are you sure?" she said, thinking that it would be a real treat for her followers.

"Yeah. As long as you still want me."

"I do! My viewers are going to love it."

"I thought we could sing our song together."

She blinked. She was thinking that he would help her cook. She had not been thinking that she would be singing on camera.

"I don't know. I don't usually sing for anyone other than my family."

"You sound amazing. And I could be wrong, but I think we sound really great together."

There was something about the way he said that that made her heart smile hugely. And something warm and sweet bloomed in her stomach.

Still, she wasn't sure how she felt about singing in front of people.

"I don't want to push you into anything you don't want to do. You've been very considerate about not pushing me into doing anything. After all, it would have been very easy for you to say that I could pay you back by doing this. And we both know I owe you."

"You don't owe me anything." Their feet crunched in the snow as the soft sound of snowflakes swirled in the air around them. "I don't think that is a normal thing anymore, but I believe, as Christians, we're supposed to do things for people and not expect anything in return. I'm not talking about just little silly things that don't mean anything. We're so unwilling to give our time to people, we're so easily angered when we do something for someone and they don't return the favor. When they don't thank us, or they don't pay us, or whatever. Like whatever happened to just being nice for the sake of being nice? Nowadays, you do that and the world calls you a doormat."

"I never really thought about that until I was here. Because I was that way. I expected people to do tit for tat. If I did something nice for you, I expected something nice in return. I expected people to pay me somehow. And here, with you, there just isn't anything of the kind. You're kind just for the sake of being kind. That's so unusual."

"It's the right thing," she said, knowing she was insisting and wishing she would have kept her mouth closed. Even if it was the right thing, she didn't always have to be right.

They walked in silence for a bit, and then he said, "Thank you for encouraging me to be a part of your family. When I'm with you guys, I truly do feel like I'm a part."

"There are so many of us, it would be kind of hard to not include people, you know? I mean, if there were only two or three of us, I think someone might have a tendency to feel left out. But with there being so many of us, there's just always a place. I don't understand how that works exactly, but I've seen it happen a lot."

"It's what's happened with me," he said.

They had reached her cabin, and she stepped up on the porch, stomping her boots to get the snow off of them.

"Thanks so much for walking home with me. Do you mind texting me when you get to your place, just so I know you got there?"

"I can do that." He grinned. "Are you worried about me?"

"A little. I don't really want to find your body in the snow somewhere tomorrow." And then, she didn't say it, but the thought came in her head that she didn't really want him to leave.

She could invite him in. There was no reason why she couldn't. Maybe it wasn't a good idea since the kids weren't there, and she always felt like it was best to be above board with things and to not be alone with a man she wasn't married to. But it wasn't like she and Cooper were in a relationship where she needed to make sure that nothing inappropriate happened. He hadn't even held her hand, kissed her. There wasn't anything inappropriate going on.

"Would you like to come in so we can practice the song that we'll sing tomorrow?" she asked with her hand on the doorknob, then she turned and faced him. "You don't have to if you don't want to. I just thought you might want to."

That wasn't true. She shook her head.

"No. I'm sorry. I just wanted you to come in. The idea of you leaving is...sad." There. She was being honest.

She had dropped her eyes, but she looked up after she spoke and saw his eyes widen, like she surprised him. That was not what she wanted to do. She didn't want him to step back away from her because he thought that her feelings were getting too strong for him. He was probably used to overzealous fans who thought they were in love with him.

She wasn't in love with him.

Was she? She wasn't even sure what that meant exactly. She loved spending time with him, looked forward to him coming, dreaded him leaving, and cherished the time they got to spend together. She thought about him all the time and was tempted to reach out and touch him at the oddest times.

"I don't want to leave you either. The more time I spend with you, the more time I want to spend."

There. He felt something too. What did that mean? Where were they going? Did she have to know?

"So, yes. If you're offering, I'll definitely come in."

"I'm offering," she said, trying to sound cheerful and unaffected but figuring that she probably failed miserably.

She stepped into the house and took her boots off beside the door. He followed suit, and she said, "Would you like something hot to drink? Coffee? Hot chocolate?"

"I'd take some hot chocolate," he said.

"Sounds like you haven't had hot chocolate for a while," she said, catching something in his tone, making her think that it had been a while.

"I think the last time I had hot chocolate was when we had an unusual snowfall in Virginia and Grandma made it. I must've been ten or twelve."

"It sounds like your grandma knew how to make snow special," she said as she moved into the kitchen, wanting to know everything there was about him but also knowing that could be a dangerous thing. He wasn't staying. He had said nothing about making a life here or wanting anyone in his life. Plus, she came with two children, and she was not going to fall for someone who wasn't going to stick around and be a father to her kids. She wasn't going to uproot her children's lives from the farm. She just wasn't. She'd waited too long to have what she did with her family and her kids.

But what if God wanted her to?

She tried to quiet that voice that always asked the questions she didn't want to ask herself. Because she knew the answer to that. She had to be willing to give up everything, anything, whatever God wanted her to give up. But surely He wouldn't ask her to give up her family?

Even as she thought it, the verse that said that a person had to be willing to give up father and mother and parents in order to follow Jesus came into her mind. It wasn't that Jesus wanted anyone to give those things up, they just had to be willing.

Sorry, Lord. I want to hold my family especially tightly to me. And I feel like that's a good thing. But I want Your will far more than I want my own, in theory, because I know Your will is always better than mine.

She continuously fought against doing what God wanted, but if she could, she would do it, even if it wasn't what she wanted or thought was best. Because how could anything be better than what God wanted?

"Family was really important to my grandma too. She taught me to make it important to myself, but I realized after spending time with your family that I hadn't lived that at all." He paused with a hand on the counter, watching as she poured packages of hot chocolate into empty cups after she put the water on the stove to boil. "Last night after we came home, I called my sister and my brother. I hadn't talked to either one of them in months. Actually, I hadn't talked to my brother in years. I credit you for inspiring me to reach out. You and your family. Thank you."

"You're welcome." His words had made her glow. She knew she

didn't deserve the credit, though. "Maybe you just got away from all the busyness of your life, and you're better able to hear the prompting of the Holy Spirit. I can't take credit for prompting you to talk to your siblings."

"You showed me the relationship that you have with your siblings. How important that is to you. How much you love the simple things." He didn't mean that in an insulting way. He moved a hand, indicating her cabin. "A lot of people would be angling for more. Bigger, better, you can never have too much, right? But you... You are content here and thrilled just to be with your family. It made me realize that all the money that I might have made, all the fame I had, all the accolades, everything, it wasn't really worth anything, because I had no one to share it with."

"That's awesome. I'm sure your family is going to be very happy being back in your life." She smiled up at him and then went over to the stove because the water was almost boiling.

"Thank you," he said as she put a spoon in his mug and slid it across the counter to him.

"I just realized you don't have your guitar. We can hardly practice if your guitar is at your cabin."

"I'll be sure to bring it in the morning." He took a breath, stirring his hot chocolate and seeming to be thinking. "I told you about everything that happened last summer, and how I had trust issues, and how I never wanted to do that again. But I find myself being drawn to you. I just wondered if you were maybe feeling the same?"

Her breath caught. She had been thinking earlier along those lines. She couldn't lie, but she didn't really want to tell him how she felt when she didn't know where it was going. She could be honest about that.

She deliberately took her hand off her spoon and set both hands flat on the counter, trying to gather her words before she looked up at him. "I... I don't want to do anything that will jeopardize my children. I don't want to be in a relationship with anyone who is not looking at marriage and family really hard. The idea of dating just for the kicks is something that I'm not interested in."

Then she felt like a fool. He wasn't talking about dating, or marriage, or anything. He was just saying he was drawn to her. Maybe he wasn't even saying that he felt anything toward her romantically. "I'm not sure what you were saying. And I'm sorry if I jumped the gun. I definitely do feel drawn to you, but I feel like it's dangerous for me to say anything or to act on any of my feelings without being on the same page as you."

She slid her hands off the counter, holding them to her sides, before shoving them in her pockets and looking up at him. "I'm not trying to push you into anything. I understand you've been through some really difficult times. I have too. And I totally get being scared to trust again. I guess I'm just telling you how things are with me. Because now that I've been married, now that I have children, everything has changed, and my priorities are for my children."

Lord, I really want to tell him I don't want to leave the farm, but I'm not going to. I'm going to trust You, and if this relationship is meant to work, it has to work on Your terms. If he wants me to leave the farm, I'm going to do it.

She wanted to say that there was no chance she was going to start a relationship if he wanted her to move somewhere else. That was how she felt. But she also knew that if the Lord wanted her to be with this man, she couldn't put parameters of her own. Of course, Cooper might ask what she thought. That would be different.

"Thank you for being upright and honest with me. I appreciate that." He seemed a little surprised.

"I'm not Regina Blue," she said, feeling the need to point that out to him.

"No. You're not. You are far more giving, and you've taught me more about sacrificing for others than Regina ever could. She's a study in selfishness."

"I'm selfish too. I really am. Maybe you haven't seen it, but it's there."

"I think humans will be dealing with selfishness for as long as they live. But you can trust me when I say you're nothing like Regina Blue."

"Why do you say her first and last name every time you talk about her?" she asked, knowing that had nothing to do with the conversation but curious nonetheless.

"I don't know. That's just how I think of her. Maybe it is to put a little distance between us. You know? You call someone by their first name when you feel close to them. But you use their first and last when they're more of an acquaintance. Regina Blue and I were never a long-term couple, despite what the tabloids said, and maybe I just wanted to make sure that it stayed that way. I don't know." He grinned at her, and she smiled back. "Any other questions, Priscilla?"

The way he said her name sent shivers down her back, and she knew he was saying it on purpose. Just to let her know that there was a big difference between her and Regina Blue.

"No, Cooper, I don't. Not about that anyway."

"You have questions?"

"Not questions you can answer. Just questions about how things are going to go. I like to be prepared, you know? And I feel like it's my responsibility to be prepared, now that I have children. I need to make sure that I'm making decisions that are beneficial to them. But I also need to make sure that I'm trusting the Lord. And sometimes when you do that, all your questions are not answered. Sometimes they're not ever answered, and sometimes they're not answered until you no longer need an answer." She paused for a moment, as though thinking. "I think God delights in doing that. Because it shows that we have faith. That we trust. I think so many people say that they have faith and that they trust God, then they try to take their life and wrest it from Him and get all the answers, and they're not content to just rest in Him, knowing that He will care for them."

"That was beautiful," he said, "and I agree with you." He drank the last of his hot chocolate and put his mug down on the counter. "I think I better go."

"Okay," she said, trying not to sound too disappointed.

"So...we established the fact that you have feelings for me the same way I have feelings for you?"

"I don't know if it's the same."

"Okay. I guess I can take that. I just... I want a little more from you, a little more with you. But I don't know if I want everything, and it sounds to me like you do want everything, and I need to think about that."

She tried not to let her heart sink into her feet, but that's where it felt like it wanted to go. He wasn't all in. He didn't know for sure if he liked her that much. Enough to talk about marriage. It was disappointing, but at least he was respecting what she had said that she didn't want to have a relationship just for the sake of having a relationship.

"Thank you for being honest with me," she said, even though that was hard. She really could go without that kind of honesty, except she couldn't. She wanted to know he was as serious as she was.

"I think you might have taken that wrong," he said, his eyes narrowing a bit as he turned away from her. "I definitely have strong feelings, no question. But I don't know for sure if I can tell you that my strong feelings are strong enough to sustain a marriage."

"I guess maybe I disagree about that. I don't think any strong feelings are strong enough to sustain a marriage. Wasn't it Dietrich Bonhoeffer who said that people try to get their feelings to sustain a marriage when it's a marriage that should sustain their feelings?"

He looked a little confused, like he didn't understand, and then he nodded. "Hm. You might be right."

She knew she was right. But she also knew that insisting that she was right didn't make other people think she was any more right. Something she was learning as she got older.

"I'll text you when I walk in the door."

"Thank you. I appreciate that consideration."

"I wouldn't want you going out in the storm looking for me."

"I'm going to give you thirty minutes to get there, and then I'm going to be going out looking." She smiled. He already knew that she cared about him, so she supposed it shouldn't surprise him she wanted to make sure he got home safely.

"It's nice to have someone who cares. Thank you."

With that, he put his boots on, and with a wave, he walked out the door.

Her heart sank a little as he left. And there were questions swirling in her head, but they were questions she knew she wasn't going to get answers to. What did he want? What was he looking for? Was he going to stay? Were they going to be together? Could he risk marrying her? Did he think that she was digging for his wealth and his prestige, and she didn't care about him as a person? That wasn't what she wanted, but what in the world would she do if he wanted her to sign an agreement? She wasn't sure where that question came from, but she knew instinctively that she would not. She was not going to have an exit strategy for marriage. Divorce to her was not an option. If it was to him, then she supposed they would have to agree to disagree and go separate ways.

Is that the way it has to be, Lord?

It seemed like God was telling her to wait and to trust Him. Which was often the hardest thing of all. But it was always the best thing.

Chapter Nineteen

Cooper tossed and turned most of the night. Most of the problem was his struggle about the idea of wanting to be with Priscilla, but being afraid. Yes, he could admit that he was scared to death of committing to her.

After what Regina Blue had done to him, the idea of trusting someone so completely again scared him to pieces.

Then, in the wee hours of the morning, he had a radical thought that changed everything: he could just have her sign a prenuptial agreement. He could include an NDA, and at that point she would not be able to say anything about him, or get anything from him. If there was nothing along those lines available, he would be free to trust her without fear.

Somehow, the idea didn't quite sit right, but it eased his anxiety to the point that he fell asleep almost immediately, and woke up feeling mostly at peace.

But he needed to talk to Bradley who handled everything for him. So, even though it wasn't daylight yet, he pulled out his phone and punched in Bradley's contact.

It rang for what felt like forever before Bradley picked up.

"Hello?" he said, in a voice rough with sleep.

"Bradley. I need you to get me a prenuptial agreement right now, and have it include an NDA. You can email it over to me as soon as you have it ready."

There was silence on the phone, and then Bradley, who sounded like he had come completely awake, said, "You're getting married?"

"I don't know whether I am or not, but I want to be prepared for it. Maybe the NDA should be separate." He thought about that for a second. "Yeah. Make it separate. Make it like it's for a girlfriend."

"You must really love this girl," Bradley said, sarcasm dripping from every syllable. He was obviously wide awake now.

"Actually, that's the problem. I do. I am head over heels in love with her, and I'm afraid I'm going to do something completely stupid." Priscilla wasn't the kind of girl Regina Blue was, and he didn't have to worry about whether or not she was going to take advantage of him.

He knew that. Yet still, the prenuptial agreement and NDA made him feel so much better. Like he could pursue a relationship with her, like he could go there today and tell her that he could be totally in. Just like she wanted him to. Because she didn't want to be with someone who wasn't serious about marriage. But what said "serious about marriage" more than a prenup, right? He could show her that he was dead serious about moving onto the next step, and he could do it without fear of being backstabbed or sold to the proverbial wolves, which just basically meant throwing their dirty laundry - when they had some - out on the Internet.

"Are you sure about this? I don't think that this is going to go over very well with any kind of girl who actually likes you for you."

Now Bradley's voice held caution, almost as though he didn't want to send Cooper into a tailspin, but he didn't think that Cooper was being very smart.

Cooper ignored the warning. "I'm sure about it. This is exactly what I need to do in order to move forward."

The words were said with confidence, but the whole time there was a part of him that was saying that he was making a huge mistake and really insulting Priscilla, who had been nothing but honest and upright with him.

That a prenup and a NDA would be a slap in the face.

Except, Priscilla wasn't the kind of woman who would not be unkind. She would understand. She would totally get why he needed to do what he was doing. In fact, he could almost see her insisting on him doing it.

With that thought, he said a few more words to Bradley, and then hung up, eager to go see the woman he couldn't stop thinking about. He was so excited, he almost forgot to take his guitar.

The idea that the world was going to get to see them together for the first time, and was going to get to hear them sing one of his songs together, put a spring in his step as he pushed through the foot of snow that had fallen overnight.

Ezra had said he would come plow them out, but he hadn't made it yet, and the world was pristine and perfect, with nothing marring the absolute beauty of the glistening white around him.

For a moment he lost his bearings a bit, but then he saw one of the stakes that had been pounded into the side of the road, probably so that whoever plowed would know where the road was. He hadn't thought to wonder why the stakes were there, but he could see the purpose now.

Still, even thinking about something as mundane as plowing snow couldn't dampen his enthusiasm, and he was knocking on Priscilla's door just as the first glistening rays of the sun started sparkling over the eastern terrain.

She had told him he could come as early as he wanted to, because she would be up early, working on some things.

Sure enough, there were lights on in her cabin, and she opened the door almost immediately after he knocked.

"It's a beautiful morning," she said in greeting.

He could smell hot chocolate, and he smiled. A feeling of happiness filling him from the bottom of his soul clear to his bones. Like he was floating instead of standing on her porch.

"It is."

"I thought you would complain that it was cold or something."

"Is it cold? I hadn't noticed," he said, stepping in as she opened the door wider, setting his guitar down, and toeing his boots off in the area right by the door.

"It's minus three," she said laughing.

"I guess I was too busy thinking about someone, and didn't even notice. I suppose I should have dressed a little warmer."

"You could have put something over your face, but I think you're probably acclimated, and you look like you managed just fine."

"My hands aren't even cold." He took a breath. "I thought of you all night."

Her eyes opened wide, and she glanced up from where she was pouring a package of hot chocolate into a mug.

"I had a little trouble getting to sleep myself. A certain handsome singer kept coming to mind."

Their eyes met across the distance, and they held there. He wanted to walk over, wanted to put his arm around her, wanted to tell her that he had made some major decisions overnight, but she moved, turning to the refrigerator and pulling out the leftover turkey.

"I decided that we're going to make Buffalo chicken pizza, only we're going to use leftover turkey. We're going to alter the recipe just a bit, since the turkey is already cooked."

They could do the video first. After that, he'd have plenty of time to talk to her, to tell her how he felt, and what he wanted and what he had decided.

"Regardless how you alter the recipe, that sounds really good," he said, coming over and standing in front of the counter, setting his guitar by the couch on his way over.

"I'll get my guitar out, so that we're ready to sing. I assume you'll edit the video some?"

He had seen online where she did a live stream basically, but other videos seemed like they had been edited.

"Yes. I wasn't going to do anything live today. I thought it might be too much pressure for you." She was quiet for a minute as she studied his face. "Are you sure you haven't changed your mind? It's not too late, you know. I can tell people things didn't work out."

"No. In fact, a live stream would be just fine with me. I am completely committed." He meant that in more ways than one, but he wasn't quite ready to tell her. They needed to get through the video first.

But his words made her smile. "All right then. I know that my followers prefer the livestream."

"Let's give them what they want. The idea is to get as many views as possible?"

"I suppose. Views, comments, and having it spread. The more I get, the more I make."

"Then let's do it. We might as well be committed."

He couldn't wait to tell her what he had decided, couldn't wait to let her know that he wanted to spend the rest of his life with her, and that they could have a relationship with that in mind.

"I'll need you to stand here on the other side of the counter. I already have my stand and camera set up. I'll just need to click a few buttons to get us started."

"All right." He moved around the counter, brushing her arm with his as they passed.

He smiled down at her, and noticed that her cheeks were red.

She was so kind, so different than the people he was usually around. And she had the values that he used to have but lost somewhere along the way. He wanted them back, and he wanted Priscilla to be beside him. Knowing that she would keep him grounded in the way he wanted and needed.

He just hoped he could be for her whatever it was that she wanted and needed.

"All right. I'm clicking the button and then we're live."

He was comfortable behind the camera, and smiled easily as she walked toward him.

He didn't exactly premeditate his gesture, but as she came closer, he put an arm around her, and drew her to his side.

He flustered her a bit, because she hemmed and hawed a little before she began to speak with confidence into the camera, welcoming her viewers and telling everyone that they were going to be making buffalo chicken pizza, which was something they could do with their Thanksgiving turkey leftovers.

"But before I start, I want to introduce you to my friend and guest, in case you haven't already recognized him." Priscilla turned to Cooper and smiled up at him.

"This is Cooper Cordray, and he has graciously agreed to cook with me today."

"Priscilla has been giving me cooking lessons, and I've gone from barely being able to boil water, to actually being able to possibly feed myself in case I should ever need to. Although, I'm hoping that I'll have Priscilla around to cook for me for a long time."

He looked down into her eyes as he said it, and hers opened wide, and then they narrowed slightly as though she were trying to figure out what exactly he was trying to say. Maybe she was putting his odd actions together, the shoulder brush, putting his arm around her, and now saying that he wanted to be with her for a long time.

"After we're done cooking, Cooper's been working on some new songs this fall and we have one that we'd like to perform for you," Priscilla said, seeming to forget that she needed to turn back and look toward the camera.

He smiled at how cute she was, and realized that anyone who was watching could probably see the adoration on his face.

Did it matter? Because, as soon as the camera was off, he was going to tell her how he felt. Was going to say that what she wanted was exactly what he wanted to give, and maybe by then Bradley would even have sent the NDA, and perhaps even the prenup. They could look them over together, and make sure that everything was good. And then, they were free to totally pursue their relationship, and Priscilla would know that he was serious about marriage.

They put the pizza together, and it didn't take long at all. He was rather surprised that he had ever thought cooking was hard.

Or maybe it was just Priscilla who made it easy.

Shortly they were sticking pizza in the oven and moving to the couch to sing while it cooked.

"This is a song that I wrote this fall like Priscilla said," he said, as she adjusted the camera and then moved around so that she sat down beside him.

"I found that there is no one in the world I'd rather sing with than Priscilla. And I also had her in mind while I was writing the song."

Her eyes were big again because it was a love song. A song that talked about how much a man admired the woman he was with. And, it spoke of love and devotion and a relationship that lasted forever.

"Yeah, it's for you, Priscilla." He added her name, because she had mentioned before that he always used Regina Blue's first and last name. It was true. He did. That put distance between them. He didn't want any distance between Priscilla and him.

She noticed, and it made her eyes glow.

He strummed the guitar and started on the verse. She came in on the chorus, and he forgot about the camera, forgot about the prenup, forgot about everything except Priscilla, and how beautifully their voices blend together, and how he felt like that was the way their lives would blend as well. A beautiful melody with harmonies so tight it almost felt like the same thing.

As the last notes of the song faded away, and they looked into each other's eyes, he couldn't help himself, but took his hand from the guitar, and wrapped it around her neck, drawing her closer to him.

She came without protest, and his breathing grew shallow as he lowered his head and their lips touched.

She sighed, a soft sound of contentment, as her hands came up and touched his neck, her fingers cool, and he wished that the guitar wasn't between them.

He deepened the kiss, and then remembered that the camera was still running and the pizza was in the oven and this wasn't supposed to happen like this.

Still, it felt perfectly right.

He lifted his head, looking into her eyes and he said, "I love you."

She seemed a little surprised, but her face broke into a smile.

He put a finger on her lips, and then looked at the camera and said, "And that's all for today, folks." He stood, setting his guitar to the side, and went and pushed the stop button on her phone.

"I'm sorry. You totally took me by surprise," she said, sounding breathless, as she stood and came over to him.

He smiled, opening his arms so she could step in, and she did, leaning against him, putting her head on his shoulder, as his arms came around her and held her close.

"I wanted to talk to you after we were done, and tell you what I had decided last night as I lay awake thinking about you. But I kinda forgot about the camera, and everything else as I was singing the song, because I meant the words for you. It's the way I feel."

"It was beautiful," she said.

He leaned back, putting his hands on her upper arms, and waiting until she met his eyes before he said, "I was thinking last night that you're right. I want to be serious about you. I want to be totally on board with everything, but I was scared. I'm scared because of what happened with Regina Blue, and all those things, and I knew you would understand. But then, I thought... Why not have a prenup? Why not have an NDA? That takes all of the risk, all of the fear of not being able to trust anyone, completely out of the equation, and everything will be okay."

As he spoke, he could feel her stiffening under him, as her eyes got wide and then they narrowed, and her face closed down, and it almost looked like he had hurt her somehow.

"I thought you would understand. You know what I've been through."

"Yes. I know," she said, softly. She didn't sound upset. She definitely didn't sound angry. Maybe a little sad, or a little discouraged, but he didn't know why she would be. She didn't understand.

"What those documents will allow me to do is to completely dedicate myself to you. And there's no worries about anything. I mean, I know that you would never do anything like that, you would never betray me the way Regina Blue did —"

"Then why do you need the prenup? Why do you need an NDA? If you trust me, and you just said you did, we don't need that."

"No. Of course we don't. Because you're completely unlike her. But for my peace of mind."

She nodded. "Your peace of mind is really important to me," she said, only this time she wasn't looking in his eyes. And he didn't like the fact that she wasn't meeting his gaze. It made him feel like there was more to her words.

"I know that. I know you're the most considerate person I've ever met. And you've been through the same thing. You understand how after being burned once, it's hard to let your guard down and believe that everything could be okay again."

"I do understand," she said, again not meeting his eyes.

Somehow she had stepped back, and there was space between them now, which he didn't like. It made him feel like the physical space was a literal space between them, keeping them from being able to truly be with each other, when every time he was with Priscilla, he felt like she knew his soul better than anyone.

He wanted to feel that closeness again, but it was gone. Like she pulled the curtain closed around her heart.

"I think it's time for me to take the pizza out of the oven," she said, stepping around him and going to the kitchen.

"Priscilla? What's wrong?"

She paused for a moment as she set a hand on the counter, and then she continued to walk toward the stove.

"I am trying to process the idea of a prenuptial agreement. I kind of feel like that is a bailout. If you go into marriage with the prenup, it's like you're saying I know things are going to go south, and this is how we're going to handle it when it does. And I don't want to go into my marriage like that. But I understand that somehow the idea of having a prenup has made you feel...better."

His phone buzzed, and he glanced down at it. It was an email from Bradley, with two attachments. He assumed it was what he had asked for him to send.

But, as he processed Priscilla's words, he dimly understood that she was saying that a prenup didn't feel like a good idea to her.

"Are you saying you don't want a prenup?"

She didn't answer him right away, but bent down, opening the oven door and pulling the pizza out. It smelled amazing, and he wanted to go over, wanted to put his arm around her, wanted to pull her close again, but it was obvious that she wasn't okay with that right now.

"I guess I'm saying that it hurts my heart to think that you think you need one. And, I don't want to go into a marriage with the exit strategy already established. It makes me feel like we're not really committing to anything."

"We would still be committed to each other. It's a lifetime commitment. I would have no intention of not upholding what I vowed."

"And I have no intention of that either. So then why do we need a prenup? And what is an NDA?"

"An NDA is a nondisclosure agreement. It means you agree to not tell anybody anything about me."

She nodded, as though she were thinking, slowly, her brows bending toward each other.

"What about me?"

He opened his mouth, and then closed it again.

What about her? He wasn't thinking anything about her. She didn't have anything to protect. She wasn't the one who had been dragged all through the news. She wasn't the one with the career in the spotlight. She wasn't the one who had already suffered from someone stealing her intellectual property.

But...did that all mean that she didn't need to be protected?

It was the man's job to protect and provide for his wife. He didn't know where that thought came from, but he knew he believed it with his whole heart.

Maybe he hadn't thought this through. He'd just done what worked for him and made him feel less anxiety. He hadn't considered what would work for her.

"I guess I don't know what to say." That was the truth.

Chapter Twenty

Priscilla bit her lip.

Her first instinct was to get angry. A prenup wasn't romantic and it didn't say I trust you, or I want you, or anything even close to that. It basically said, we're going to get divorced, so let's get this figured out before we get angry at each other and fight.

And what was the point in that?

Although, a prenup would have made things a lot easier when her ex decided to cheat on her. At least they would have had it spelled out what was going to happen when he cheated, then they wouldn't have had to fight about it.

Maybe she was looking at it all wrong.

She had set the pizza on the counter, and she just stood there in the kitchen, her hands on the counter. Telling herself not to get upset. This wasn't worth getting angry over. He wasn't trying to insult her. He wasn't trying to take advantage of her. Maybe there was a perfectly logical explanation for it, and she was overreacting.

"I guess I feel like a prenup says, 'I don't trust you, and I'm not going into this thinking that we're going to stay married forever'." She turned around and looked him in the eye. She needed to handle this like an adult. She couldn't get upset and go storming off, or start screaming at him because he didn't do what she thought he should. He was a rational adult, and one she really thought a lot of...one she loved. Just because he did something she thought was completely wrong, didn't make him a bad person.

"This just did what I needed it to. It made me feel like I didn't need to worry about things anymore. I was tossing and turning last night, thinking about how I had such a hard time trusting. And then, when I thought about prenup, I realized that was all I had to do to put that totally out of my mind. It wasn't that I thought that you were going to doublecross me in any way. And it's definitely not that I think that we're going to get divorced. If I decide to get married, I'm not going to be looking for an escape route. Just...it gave me peace of mind."

"I suppose the idea of a prenup takes my peace of mind away." She paused, trying to be reasonable. "But maybe if I think about it for a little bit, I'll get used to the idea. I was... Surprised when you suggested it."

"Maybe it was a dumb suggestion. I know that you're not going to do anything, that's head knowledge. But for some reason, my heart says I can't trust anyone."

"Maybe we shouldn't have a relationship if we don't feel like we can trust each other?" She didn't want to say that. She wanted to have a relationship no matter what, and she had been prepared to even give up her family and move wherever he wanted her to, if she needed to. She hadn't been expecting this.

Lord? Am I wrong? Should I just let this go? Am I overreacting?

She wanted to be able to think rationally about it, and not allow her emotions to dictate how she acted.

But at the same time, she had never even considered being with anyone who would say that they didn't trust her to the point where they felt like they needed a prenup.

Of course, maybe he was only protecting his assets, and maybe it really did give him a peace of mind that he could move forward without fear.

"I guess you could be right. But I don't want to hear that. The idea that we couldn't have a relationship... I want one with you."

"I definitely want one with you. I don't go around kissing people randomly. And, I did that in front of a lot of people." She hadn't even considered the ramifications if they broke it off now. Of course, it was certainly better to not be with someone who didn't trust her, then to waste a lot of time with someone who was never going to believe that she wasn't the kind of person who would steal things from him for her own benefit.

"I think until we figure this out, it's best if my children don't know. They're not on social media, and I'll try to make sure they don't see this episode...." Although she knew they were going to ask about it. Maybe she should delete it.

She touched the phone in her back pocket. "I think I might go ahead and delete it."

"I really don't want you to." His words were spoken softly, but firmly. He meant them.

"I don't want my kids to see me kissing someone that...we're not together. It's setting a really bad example. Although... I guess I did it, and I can't hide all of my mistakes from them."

His face winced when she said "mistakes". She didn't mean to hurt him, but if they weren't going to have a long-term relationship, she definitely considered kissing him a mistake. Didn't she?

But it had felt so right.

But she didn't live by her feelings.

"I don't want your kids to see that either if it's going to hurt you or them. I certainly don't want to do anything to cause them any kind of pain. That has never been my goal or aim."

"I know. I know you wouldn't hurt them, and you definitely wouldn't hurt me. You're a good man. That's part of the reason I love you. I guess I didn't say that earlier, and now I feel like maybe I shouldn't. I should just keep that bottled up, especially if we're not going to be together, but it's true. I do. Love you. But, I don't know if it's a good idea for us to try to make this work if we have such different feelings about it."

He had moved from where he stood beside the couch, staring at her, his shoulders slumped, looking about as miserable as a man could look. Her heart went out to him, and she wished there was something she could do to make it better, but other than telling him a prenup would be fine, and an NDA would be perfectly okay as well, she didn't know what else she could say. And then, she realized that, if she were completely committed, and she felt like he was too, because she believed him when he said he was, if a prenup gave him a piece of mine, none of it should bother her.

"Priscilla, I –"

She put a hand up. "It's okay. I actually just figured it out. A prenup doesn't mean anything if we don't get divorced, and I have zero plans for that. I don't think you do either, and it gives you peace of mind. So it's a nonissue. The NDA is a nonissue as well. I had no plans to say anything about you that you didn't want me to. I certainly wouldn't want to run my mouth and hurt you. So, give me your documents, and I'll sign them."

"No. I guess things just clicked for me too. You're not Regina Blue. You're not some random person who might end up hurting me. I don't know why I was even considering this last night. Except, I guess sometimes in the middle of the night things make sense but when you run them out in the harsh light of day, you realize that you're being dumb."

She laughed. "You weren't being dumb. You were trying to protect yourself."

"But, I wasn't protecting you, and that's what I'm supposed to do. It's my job."

"I think your job is to sing, isn't it?"

He shook his head. "No. If you and I are together, my job is to protect and to provide for you. And, even if we get divorced, I would want to make sure that you are provided for. But," he held up his hand when she started to open her mouth. "I don't want to ever utter that word again. From my perspective, there is no such thing as divorce. It's just you and me, together forever." He smiled. "I used to think music was my big dream, but my big dream is not music. It's family. Family like yours, where we love each other and get along and hang out and have fun. I don't know if it'll be okay for us to live here forever, but I love this place, and I don't want to leave it."

"What about your career?" she asked, taking a step toward him, hope blossoming in her heart.

"I was kind of thinking that you have your social media channels. You already have a foundation, maybe we can just build on those."

"On mine?"

"Sure. We did our debut together today. We can cook together, we can sing together, and...who knows."

"Won't you miss singing in front of people?"

"I wouldn't say I would never do it again, but I told you, I realize now that's not my big dream. You are."

How could she go from feeling so miserable just a few minutes ago, to being the happiest woman in the world now?

She wasn't quite sure exactly how that could happen, but she knew it had.

"I guess I don't care. I'm happy and content here or anywhere, as long as I'm with you. I suppose that's what I was thinking about last night when I couldn't sleep."

"What's that?" he asked, walking slowly toward her and sliding his arms around her waist, pulling her close.

She looked up at him. "I was afraid that being with you would mean I would have to leave my family. And I didn't want to. I love it here."

"I don't want you to leave your family. This is part of what I love about you. How you are so devoted to them. The way you work to get along so your kids can have a great upbringing. You remind me so much of my grandma in a lot of ways, in the very best ways."

"But I decided it didn't matter. If it was God's will for me to be with you, then I had to follow you no matter where you went. Whether that was here, or somewhere else."

"You would have given up your family for me?"

She nodded. "If that's what I needed to do. If we're going to be together, and you can't do what you need to do here, then I need to be with you. Because, if I'm your wife, that's my place."

He grinned a little, and she could feel her cheeks heating. He hadn't asked her to marry him.

"You decided you would give up everything you love for me, and I decided that I needed a prenup. I am embarrassed at the different conclusions we came to. Obviously, you were right."

"No. You just did what you needed to in order to make yourself feel at peace."

"All I needed to do was think about how trustworthy you were, and then I would have felt the peace I needed." He brushed his knuckles over her cheekbone, and threaded his fingers into her hair. "I'm sorry. I'm sorry that my comfort and my safety were the only things I was thinking about last night. I should've been spending my time thinking about how I could make you comfortable. Make you feel safe. Protect you and provide for you and be the man you deserve."

"You don't have to try to do that. You already are. Far more than I deserve."

"I guess we'll just have to agree to disagree on that," he said. His head started to lower. "Although, I don't really want to talk about it right now. I kinda like that whole kissing thing we started earlier, and I wanted to try again."

"That's funny. I was thinking the exact same thing."

She lifted her head, and he kissed her. Or, she kissed him. She wasn't quite sure which, but it was very, very good.

Join Jessie's list and be the first to know about new releases and sales on her books!

Read *A Cowboy's Convenient Marriage*, a deeply romantic journey of two hearts brought together by circumstance—and held together by something far stronger. Ada Clyborne never imagined her walk down the aisle would be for anything less than love, but the quiet strength in Cash Johnson stirs feelings she never expected. As their simple arrangement begins to blossom into something real, could a marriage of convenience turn into the love story they both stopped believing was possible?

"I'm sorry, but we have no choice but to ask you to clean out your desk and vacate the property."

Pastor Cash Johnson stared in disbelief at his head deacon.

He couldn't believe it. They were going to fire him from the church that he had started? And pastored for the last decade?

He managed to find his tongue. "But her allegations are untrue. Doesn't that mean anything?"

"I'm sorry. There's really no way for us to know the truth for sure since it's your word against hers. But if we want to save the church, if we want to continue to have a congregation, we have to do something. You know if we let this go, folks will leave the church in droves. No matter what the truth is, people aren't going to trust you after this."

"But I'm the same person I always was," he said, surprised at how calm his voice sounded. There was a peace in his soul that had to come from the Lord, because he certainly was not expecting to have this happen this morning.

"I know that." John Boxer met his gaze steadily. "But a pastor has to avoid any hint of impropriety. You've said that often enough yourself."

Cash pressed his lips closed. He had said that. And he had broken his own rule.

"Do you believe her?" he asked, not even sure exactly what Zoe Newson was even accusing him of.

"We were good friends since before you were even a pastor. I knew you in college. And we went to high school together. You're the most upright man I know. I don't believe for a second what she's saying is true. But I also know that over my lifetime, I've seen people do things I would never have believed that they could possibly do. Surely you see the best thing for the church is for you to go?"

Cash could see that. If it were another pastor in his position, he would be saying the same thing. But it was him. And he knew he was being honest when he said he had done nothing inappropriate with this girl who was accusing him of...he wasn't even sure.

"What exactly did she say I did?" he asked, his whole inside feeling like it was melting down, but his voice was still calm. Maybe it was the peace of the Lord, or maybe it was just the fact that he was shocked and hadn't really had this sink in. He felt a little bit like God had abandoned him just now. After blessing pretty much every single thing that he had done for the last fifteen years.

It was the first time John broke eye contact. He looked down and shifted, almost as though he were embarrassed to even speak the words out loud. "She said the two of you had been developing a relationship for a while. And she said you had a sexual relationship for the last month or so. She detailed times and places where you two... you know." John looked distinctly uncomfortable and shifted in his chair.

"No, I don't know. I didn't do anything. There was no intimate relationship." And for the first time, Cash could hear the anger coming out in his voice. "There was no relationship at all."

"I'm not arguing with you. Although I did see with my very own eyes you standing at a basketball game with your arm around her, and then you gently led her toward the door. There was definitely tenderness in your touch. At the time—"

"She came to me crying! What was I supposed to do? Shove her to the ground?" He hadn't wanted to touch her. It was his policy that he didn't touch women. This was the exact reason, so that there was never any hint of impropriety. The Bible said to avoid all appearance of evil, and for his own personal standards, he took that a little further. Because he had never wanted to be in this exact position.

"Of course not. I didn't think at the time there was anything going on at all. But in light of these new accusations, I'm just telling you what I saw. Other people saw it too."

"It was a gymnasium full of people. I wasn't hiding anything."

John didn't say anything, but he didn't need to. He'd already said that Cash and Zoe were heading toward the door. That's because Zoe had told him she needed to go outside. She claimed she got in a huge fight with her best friend and that her best friend had said that she was going to attack her in the parking lot. That's why Cash had walked out with her, making sure she got safely to her car.

Come to think of it, Zoe had turned around, keeping a hold of him and trying to hug him.

He had extracted himself with some difficulty and told her to drive safely. Then he called her parents and let them know that she was upset and on her way home. He hadn't followed through; in hindsight, he wished he would have. But in the amount of time he'd spent in the ministry, teenage girls were notoriously emotional and difficult. He had just chalked it up to that exact thing.

"So I don't even get a chance to clear my name? I can prove that none of her accusations are true."

He really couldn't prove anything hadn't happened behind closed doors, and there was one time where Zoe had walked into his office and shut the door and he hadn't jumped up from his desk and run around and opened the door. He should have. He wished he would have, but he hadn't. Now, the one time in his ministry where he'd allowed himself to be in a potentially compromising situation, it turned out that all of the work that he put into keeping his life and reputation aboveboard was going to be for naught.

Lord? How could You do this to me? How could You allow this to happen? Aren't I serving You faithfully? Aren't we seeing souls saved and lives changed in this ministry? Aren't I giving You all the glory? I'm not driving around the country, tooting my own horn, writing books, and making millions. I'm pouring my heart and soul into this ministry You gave me and doing everything I can to serve the people here.

That was when his heart cracked. He loved the people of his congregation. He'd prayed for years that God would give him love, fervent and strong, for every single person who set foot in his church. God answered that prayer in ways Cash couldn't even explain. Just by thinking about how much God loved him, spending hours every month meditating on God's great love for him, picturing God looking at him in love, just those small things had completely changed his heart and attitude toward others and in particular the people of his church.

The idea of leaving them made him want to double over. It hurt even worse than the accusations of wrongdoing and the knowledge that even his head deacon and best friend, John Boxer, did not believe in his innocence enough to fight for him.

"I'm sorry, Cash. You can't prove what didn't happen behind closed doors. And the board must take this girl's accusations seriously. The police are going to be involved; she's underage. Our church is going to be dragged through the mud. The only thing that can possibly save us is for us to completely cut ties with you the second we hear about it. For us to even entertain the idea that you could stay on and we would fight this makes it look like we're condoning that behavior. You know how this goes. The woman is always right."

Even when she was dead wrong.

It was so unfair.

He knew that there were many people who hated the Lord and did not want to see anything good happen in any church, who would jump on this and ride it hard, criticizing anyone who dared defend a man who would take advantage of a young girl. He would be tarred and feathered and strung up metaphorically before the first newscast was over.

John was right. The only way to save the church and the work he had carried out for the Lord for the last decade or so was for him to immediately remove himself from any association with it.

The thought hurt, but it was the only course of action that could potentially not just save the church but help it to grow. People would know that this church, while holding onto biblical principles, also kept those in the ministry accountable and protected the young and innocent. It was possible that people would actually be drawn to the church instead of leaving it in droves like John had just been talking about.

Maybe if they hadn't just borrowed four million dollars and were almost finished with the construction of a brand-new sanctuary and activity center, which would be big enough to hold two thousand people in the sanctuary and five thousand people in the bleachers of the activity center, maybe he would try to hang on. But if the church defaulted on that loan, they would lose the building and their congregation.

Sign up for Jessie's newsletter! Get a free book, access to exclusive bonus content, get fun and funny updates on her life on the farm and more!

A Gift from Jessie

View this code through your smart phone camera to be taken to a page where you can download a FREE ebook when you sign up to get updates from Jessie Gussman! Find out why people say, "Jessie's is the only newsletter I open and read" and "You make my day brighter. Love, love, love reading your newsletters. I don't know where you find time to write books. You are so busy living life. A true blessing." and "I know from now on that I can't be drinking my morning coffee while reading your newsletter – I laughed so hard I sprayed it out all over the table!"

Claim your free book from Jessie!

Escape to more faith-filled romance series by Jessie Gussman!

The Complete Sweet Water, North Dakota Reading Order:

Series One: Sweet Water Ranch Western Cowboy Romance (11 book series)

Series Two: Coming Home to North Dakota (12 book series)

Series Three: Flyboys of Sweet Briar Ranch in North Dakota (13 book series)

Series Four: Sweet View Ranch Western Cowboy Romance (10 book series)

Spinoffs and More! Additional Series You'll Love:

Jessie's First Series: Sweet Haven Farm (4 book series)

Small-Town Romance: The Baxter Boys (5 book series)

Bad-Boy Sweet Romance: Richmond Rebels Sweet Romance (3 book series)

Sweet Water Spinoff: Cowboy Crossing (9 book series)

Small Town Romantic Comedy: Good Grief, Idaho (5 book series)

True Stories from Jessie's Farm: Stories from Jessie Gussman's Newsletter (3 book series)

Reader-Favorite! Sweet Beach Romance: Blueberry Beach (8 book series)

Blueberry Beach Spinoff: Strawberry Sands (10 book series)

From Strawberry Sands to: Raspberry Ridge (12 book series)

Swoonfully Jolly Holiday Stories:

Holiday Romance: Cowboy Mountain Christmas (6 book series)

Cowboy Mountain Christmas Spinoff: A Heartland Cowboy Christmas (9 book series)

New and Much Loved: Mistletoe Meadows (4 books and counting!)

Laughing Through the Snow: Christmas Tree, PA Sweet Romcoms (6 short reads)